'I hope you got those instructions the right way round,' David said after firing a barrage of them at her. 'You'd better read them back to me.'

Jacqui flinched at the reminder of her slip in remembering the directions she'd been given at the service station, but kept calm and said, 'Certainly.' To her relief, she had got down everything he had said correctly.

Finally he stood up to go. He stood for a moment looking down at her, then, hands on the desk, leaning towards her, he said, 'You don't have to wear a hair shirt forever because you bashed my bumper yesterday. I've quite forgiven you!'

Jacqui felt her face flame. 'So what am I supposed to do now?' she demanded. 'Go down on bended knee and say thank you very much?'

A low, throaty chuckle reverberated round the room. 'I can tell that red hair is the real thing! We shall have to watch our step around here.'

Judith Worthy lives in an outer suburb of Melbourne, Australia, with her husband. When not writing she can usually be found bird-watching or gardening. She also likes to listen to music and the radio, paints a little, likes to travel and is concerned about conservation and animal cruelty. As well as romantic fiction she also writes books for children.

Previous Titles

LOCUM LOVER
HEART SPECIALIST
DOCTOR IN PRACTICE

DOCTOR DARLING

BY

JUDITH WORTHY

MILLS & BOON LIMITED
ETON HOUSE   18–24 PARADISE ROAD
RICHMOND   SURREY   TW9 1SR

*First published in Great Britain 1990
by Mills & Boon Limited*

© Judith Worthy 1990

*Australian copyright 1990
Philippine copyright 1990
This edition 1990*

ISBN 0 263 76910 0

*Set in 10 on 12 pt Linotron Times
03-9008-49948
Typeset in Great Britain by Centracet, Cambridge
Made and printed in Great Britain*

CHAPTER ONE

'WELL, that's the lot, I think. Phew!'

Jacqueline Brent sat heavily on the edge of the suitcase and fastened the catches. Her usually smooth brow was furrowed and her lips pursed with the effort. Cheeks flushed, she looked triumphantly up at her flatmate. 'If I've left anything behind, Lissa, you can have it!' She glanced at the other two bulging cases and sighed. 'Obviously I'm a squirrel at heart. No peripatetic nurse should acquire so many material possessions!' She jumped up and shifted the case she had been sitting on into line with the others.

'I wish you weren't doing this,' Lissa Moran said anxiously. 'You were so *settled* here, Jacqui.'

Jacqui wove her fingers into the cascade of copper-bright hair that tumbled in shining waves around her shoulders and lifted the tresses in a slightly nervous gesture. She wasn't a hundred per cent sure she was doing the right thing herself.

'I have to do something,' she said through gritted teeth. 'I can't stand being where everyone *knows*. And when his case comes up, imagine the whispers, the sly looks, the sniggers.'

'You're being hypersensitive,' insisted Lissa. 'Everybody is sympathetic. It's not as though you were in any way involved.'

'No—just hoodwinked and humiliated.' Jacqui flopped into an armchair and swung her long jean-clad legs over the arm. She contemplated her orchid-pink

5

toenails and reached out to scratch a flake of varnish off one of them. 'And maybe I am being over-sensitive. But for most people, where there's smoke there's fire, and the fact is, Lissa, I can't seem to concentrate as I used to. I feel I'm being stared at and talked about even if it isn't true. I'm not working at full capacity, and I know it's going to get worse if I stay at SCG. I need to get away. . .' She trailed away as emotions she had tried not to let engulf her over the past weeks threatened to surface.

'But why take this country job? You'll never stick it, Jacqui. You're a city girl, born and bred, and you always said you'd hate to live in the country.' Lissa added, 'If you must flee, why don't you go home? That's what I would have done.'

'With my tail between my legs? My family thought I was mad coming out here in the first place. To go home now would be like admitting it was a mistake.' Jacqui shrugged. They'd been over it all before and it was too late now to change her mind. She'd accepted the job as charge nurse at a country hospital, given in her notice, and had today finished her last shift at Melbourne's South City General Hospital.

Leaving tonight at the end of her shift, she had glanced back once from the tram stop and her heart had constricted painfully. It had been a satisfying and rewarding two years at the big city hospital and she hated leaving. Tears had misted her eyes as she looked for the last time across the forecourt at the entrance, blazing with light, then up at the rows of ward windows, some curtained, some with blinds drawn, some still lit. She had flinched as always at the sound of a siren as an ambulance approached from the distance, and then her tram had arrived and carried her away with merciful swiftness.

She said, 'I was tempted, Lissa, don't worry. My first thought when I discovered what a fake Carey was, that he wasn't just a womaniser but dishonest in other ways as well, was to bolt right back to where I came from. But later, when the shock subsided, I realised that's not what I want to do.' She smiled faintly. 'Not yet. I like Australia. . . I don't want to go home yet. It would have seemed even more cowardly than what I am doing.'

She and Lissa had come out from Britain at about the same time, part of a batch of nurses who had answered advertisements for nursing posts in Melbourne. They were both Londoners, Lissa from Highgate, Jacqui from Wimbledon, and both had trained and worked in inner London hospitals. When Lissa had put a note on the staff notice-board asking for a flatmate, Jacqui had phoned her. They'd 'clicked' at once and had become firm friends. Now Jacqui felt she was walking out on her friend in a way, but she simply had to get away, or go crazy.

If only she hadn't fallen so heavily for Carey Matthews. She'd met him at a party and his smooth charm and impeccable manners had bowled her over. He was a solicitor, an ambitious man, but it had never occurred to her that under the suave but sometimes boyish charm, behind those candid blue eyes, lurked a ruthless desire to make a lot of money in a hurry.

She'd met his family and liked them; they'd become engaged, and had even begun to talk of wedding plans. And then the balloon went up. She'd discovered that Carey was seeing another woman behind her back, the daughter of a well-known property developer, but before she could confront him with it, Carey had vanished—two days before an inquiry was due to begin into what appeared to be a big land swindle.

Jacqui had been shocked and distraught and had run straight to the Matthews, sure that he couldn't possibly be involved. But the minute she saw his parents, Jacqui knew that what the papers were saying was most probably true. Mrs Matthews was sympathetic, and stoical. Reluctantly, when Jacqui had felt bound to mention it, she had revealed that she knew Carey had been about to break off his engagement to her. That had been the final straw. That had been what had hurt most, that he'd been planning to dump her, and she hadn't suspected a thing, until that little rumour about his being seen with the property magnate's daughter had reached her ears.

His mother had said sadly, 'I never expected Carey to get into this sort of trouble. I just don't understand why he did it and I don't know how his father will survive it. . .' She had added kindly, 'We'll see you don't get involved, my dear. You deserve that much at least.'

Jacqui had offered what comfort she could, but there was little she could say. Her own life had been utterly shattered, dealt a double blow that she wondered if she would ever recover from. Over and over she kept asking herself, how had she not known, how had she come to make such a grave error of judgement? She'd been so sure that Carey was solid, reliable and trustworthy. And she had turned out to be a gullible fool.

Like her own mother, she thought a trifle ruefully. Her mother had married a man who, like Carey, had immense charm, burning ambition and unfortunately an inability, it seemed, to remain faithful. Her mother had tolerated his peccadilloes until Jacqui and her two brothers were old enough to leave home, and then she had divorced him. At least, Jacqui had reminisced, her father had only been a philanderer. Lovable rogues, both of them, she supposed wryly, only Carey was not lovable any more. She still loved her father. It was impossible not to like him, not to forgive him, not to be bowled over by him. Feckless he might have been, but he had had integrity. But Carey—her affection for him had wilted and died in days, screwing up into a residual pain that lodged like a rock in her heart. She couldn't forgive him. Lissa said she'd had a lucky escape, and Jacqui supposed she had, but that didn't console her. She felt tainted by his dishonesty, as though loving him made her guilty too.

As the days passed and she was routinely interviewed by police, then Carey was located and arrested, and the whole horrible business became clearer, Jacqui knew she had to flee. Fortunately, she was not expected to appear in court, and her name had been kept out of the Press, for which she guessed she had Carey's parents, especially his barrister father, to thank. They seemed to feel a great responsibility towards her and were anxious that she should not become even peripherally involved in their son's disgrace. Consequently, no one at Lakeside, Maneroo and District Community Hospital was likely to connect Jacqui with the sensational revelations in the Mitchell Park Estate land swindle.

'You could switch to another metropolitan hospital,' Lissa said, although she knew it was too late to dissuade Jacqui from the course of action she'd chosen. She considered her friend anxiously. 'You'll miss the city. You'll be miserable, buried out there in the back of beyond in that tinpot little town with its tinpot little hospital——' Jacqui's stubborn look made her break off. 'Oh, what's the use? You're going.' She gave a rather wintry smile. 'I'll miss you, Jacqui. We've had some great times.'

'I'll miss you too, Lissa,' Jacqui said affectionately. 'And if it's any consolation, I'm a bit unsure myself whether I'm doing the right thing or not. I know I might have been a bit hasty, but truly, Lissa, I have to get right away. Another Melbourne hospital might only keep bringing me up against people I know—you know how medical staff move around—and I'd be bound to keep bumping into people outside the hospital who knew Carey and I were engaged. I already have done, and I can't bear their sympathy and their curiosity, and the slightly speculative way they look at me as though they think I might know more about it all than I'm letting on. . .'

'You're paranoid!'

'I suppose so. I just know I want time and space to build up a rational perspective, and I can't do that in Melbourne. It's affecting my work, Lissa, and that's bad. For me and for the patients.'

'Yes, I do understand,' Lissa said quietly. 'And I hope it works out for you, Jacqui. It's been a terrible strain for you and, believe me, I'm not underestimating what you've been through, are still going through.' She sighed. 'I suppose you're right to cut yourself off from everything for a while.' She mustered a grin. 'It's just that I can't see myself settling down to rural life, and I can't see you doing it either.'

Jacqui laughed wryly. 'I admit it does sound like a tall order. But at least I should be safe from romantic temptations, which will be just as well, given my apparent inability to recognise a rogue or a philanderer when I meet one!'

'There are probably fewer of those in the country,' observed Lissa naïvely. 'But you might meet some rich grazier who's already got more money than he knows what to do with.'

'If I do, I'll give him some advice on what to do with it,' said Jacqui with a laugh, 'but you needn't worry about me falling for any man again in a hurry. Besides, I'm a city girl, as you said, and I don't in any case go for those macho men from the bush in their wide-brimmed Akubras and skin-tight jeans who swagger about imitating film folk-heroes. Remember those guys we saw at the Royal Agricultural Show? No, thank you!'

'I don't think they're all like that,' Lissa said.

Jacqui headed for the kitchen. 'I'm going to make some cocoa. Want some?'

'Yes, OK.' Lissa followed her dispiritedly.

'I'll get away as early as I can in the morning,' Jacqui said. 'I'll drop you off at the hospital if you like.'

'Thanks. I'm on at seven.'

'Maggie's moving in tomorrow night?'

'I hope we hit it off,' Lissa said, frowning.

'You two'll get on fine,' Jacqui assured her friend. 'Maggie's the sort who pulls her weight, off the ward as well as on it, I'm willing to bet.'

It had been lucky that a new nurse had been looking for a flat to share at just the moment when Jacqui was looking for someone to replace herself. She had felt duty bound to find someone who would be compatible with Lissa, and had been relieved when she had agreed to share with Maggie. She would have felt terribly guilty going off and leaving her friend to carry the burden of the full rent herself.

Offering to drop Lissa off at the hospital had been, Jacqui realised next morning, an unconscious excuse to see the hospital again. It was strange, she reflected, as the main building came into view on the skyline, how quickly she had become attached to the place. At first, after her London hospital, it had all seemed very strange and she had been homesick for quite a while. But gradually, as she'd made friends, adjusted to the different routines and methods of doing things and had lost her reserve with the other nurses and medicos, the hospital had grown on her and she had felt a real sense of belonging.

Like her old London hospital, it had deeply entrenched if not as ancient traditions, and inspired immense loyalty from its staff. She had felt like a traitor leaving. The DON had been sympathetic, but obviously disappointed at her defection, and after she had given in her notice Jacqui had felt an immediate sense of loss. Despite the inevitable problems, the internal politics and occasional upheavals and industrial troubles, South City General was a warm and caring place to work, a close-knit community of people whose dedication was superlative. Although she had been as happy in her work there as at any time in her career, Jacqui had nevertheless been surprised at how painful the wrench had been when she decided to leave. But she wouldn't come running back, she told herself firmly. She turned into the forecourt and parked.

'There you go,' she said brightly to Lissa. 'Five minutes to spare!'

Lissa leaned across and kissed her cheek. 'All the

best, Jacqui. Don't forget to write or phone, will you, love?'

'I expect I'll be able to manage a visit one weekend,' Jacqui said. 'So don't throw out the air-bed.' But not yet, she thought, not until she felt more secure in herself, and the public fuss over Carey had died down. She would stay away just as long as she could.

Lissa reached into the pocket of her jacket, withdrew a small packet and pressed it into Jacqui's hand.

'What's this?'

Lissa stumbled out of the car. 'Just a little farewell gift. Look at it later. I'd better dash. Good luck, love.'

'And you. . .' Jacqui held the small tissue-wrapped packet in her hand and swallowed on a hard lump in her throat. Lissa had been such a good friend, it was a wrench leaving her, going somewhere to be among strangers again. She watched Lissa half running towards the hospital staff entrance, and again she felt keenly that she was running out on her friend, on her job, on everything.

'I'm such a coward. . .' she muttered, and if it had been possible to change her mind at that moment, she might well have done, but a car hooting its horn behind her galvanised her into action. She hurriedly placed the packet in the glove box and shot forward, swinging round to the exit gate.

Jacqui had a long drive ahead of her. She was not, by Australian standards anyway, going all that far away from Melbourne, but the fact that it was nearly as far as from London to Edinburgh made it seem a vast distance. Maneroo was a town on a lake in the north-west of the state of Victoria, near the Big Desert in the vast wheat and sheep-farming area of the Wimmera. Jacqui had not been there before.

At Ballarat she stopped briefly for a cup of coffee, and, before she took off again, opened her gift from Lissa. The small pottery owl that emerged from the green tissue paper made her both laugh and cry. A card around its neck proclaimed 'This is Mopoke—who's also missing you. Lots of love, and come back soon, from Lissa.'

It was a fitting memento. On her first night at the flat, Jacqui had been mystified by an eerie sound that seemed to be coming from a tree outside her bedroom window, and she had woken Lissa. Lissa had already discovered its origin—a small brown owl which was colloquially called a mopoke because its mournful call was a repeated *mo-poke*. Jacqui had been eager to see the creature, and after much late-night prowling with a powerful torch they had eventually spotted it perched on a branch close to Jacqui's window, looking wide-eyed and surprised at being disturbed.

Jacqui set the little pottery owl up on top of the dashboard, brushed a tear away, and set off once more. With every kilometre that took her further from Melbourne, she began to have increasing misgivings about Maneroo, the unknown country town. Lakeside Hospital was an even more daunting prospect. She had never worked in a small hospital before and now, suddenly, she was apprehensive. Would she fit in? Would they accept her as South City General had done, or would these country people be stand-offish and unfriendly? It could take a long time, she'd heard, to become accepted in many English rural communities. Maybe it would be the same here, maybe worse. She'd always heard how friendly and welcoming country Australians were, and yet. . . Alone in the car with only her thoughts for company, she grew more and more apprehensive.

She stopped for lunch at Horsham, and already she was beginning to feel intimidated by the vastness of the landscape. The picturesque rolling country she had encountered on the road to Ballarat and even beyond had, surprisingly, reminded her of the English countryside. The paddocks of wheat and other crops were green now, and there were many European trees to relieve the grey-green monotony of the gums. But soon the hills flattened out and she was travelling through a landscape that seemed to have a limitless horizon, where habitation was sparse, and the world seemed to belong to the sheep, the crows, the magpies and the flocks of colourful parrots that started up screeching from the roadside as she passed.

Off the main highway, she encountered less traffic, and the cars and trucks that did pass her going in the opposite direction mostly saluted. Jacqui soon became accustomed to returning the wave, and it was almost a game guessing whether an approaching vehicle's driver would wave or not. But at least it was reassuring, a friendly gesture that helped to allay a little of her apprehension.

She reached Maneroo in late afternoon. And, as she suddenly realised, she only just made it. She had been too preoccupied with her thoughts to notice that her petrol was running low, and as she arrived on the outskirts of the town an ominous spluttering gave her warning that she wasn't going to get much further without filling up.

There wasn't much to be seen of the town. The country was flat, and the single-storey houses sprawled over it in a seemingly haphazard fashion. There was no sign of a hospital, nor any sign pointing to it. There was also no sign of a garage. Jacqui gritted her teeth. The last thing she wanted to do was to announce her arrival by breaking down in the main street. That wouldn't exactly advertise her competence.

Just as she was about to despair, she spotted an oil company sign just ahead, on her side of the road.

'Thank goodness!' she breathed in relief, and swung the car into the service station forecourt to halt in front of a bowser. The engine died on her before she could even switch it off. A young man came out of the office, grinned amiably at her, and, when she got out to stretch her legs for a minute while he filled the tank, looked her over with full male appreciation.

'Going far?' he enquired, as she counted out the money.

'No. This is where I stop. Can you direct me to the hospital?'

'Sure.' He jerked a thumb down the main street. 'Take the first on your right, second left, and keep going down to the lake. You can't miss it. It's just beyond the caravan park and campsite.'

'Thanks.'

He looked at her curiously as though waiting for her to reveal her reason for being in Maneroo, but the question remained unasked and Jacqui did not enlighten him. He loped off to get her change. While she waited, a large dark green car drove in and pulled up by the automatic bowser behind her car. A man got out and unhooked the hose.

Jacqui let a wry smile curve her lips. He was exactly the type she had decried to Lissa. He was tall, rangy, dressed in close-fitting jeans, a check shirt and, believe it or not, a wide-brimmed felt hat. He wore boots like a cowboy, and his rather swashbuckling air made Jacqui want to laugh. She hadn't expected to encounter the stereotype so soon. He had a strong profile, though, and broad shoulders, narrow hips and muscular legs. She couldn't see what colour his eyes were, but the hair below the brim of his hat, curling up slightly on his collar, was a dark tawny colour, like wheat stubble.

Seeming to sense her scrutiny, he angled his head and looked right at her. The dying sun illluminated his face, giving his tanned features a warm glow. She still couldn't tell what colour his eyes were, but there was no doubt that as they slid over her trim figure in blue cords and white oversize T-shirt he was taking it all in.

The garage attendant returned with her change. Jacqui slid behind the wheel, glad to be out of range of the piercing look of the other customer. The garage attendant's face filled the driving window. 'Got your directions OK?'

'Yes, thanks. First left, second right and I can't miss it.'

He laughed loudly. 'No! First right, second left! The way you were going, you'd have ended up at the town tip!'

Jacqui was uncomfortably aware of the stranger watching and smiling cynically. 'Sorry,' she muttered, cursing herself for getting it wrong.

'First right, second left,' repeated the garage attendant. 'Then keep going until you see the sign. It's right on the lakeside.'

As Jacqui thanked him again, he turned to speak to the other customer, who apparently wanted something from the shop. As they walked away, Jacqui heard the telephone in the office ringing. The garage attendant hurried ahead while the other customer paused and looked back at her. For some reason this flustered her. She fumbled as she started the engine and put the car into first gear. At least that was what she thought she'd done. What happened was totally unexpected. The car went into reverse with a sudden jerky movement, and before Jacqui could prevent it there was a sickening crunch of metal on metal. She had rammed the car behind her.

Face scarlet, she got out, to see the Akubra-hatted cowboy striding towards her, his face like thunder.

'What in the name of heaven do you think you're doing?' he demanded, glaring at her. 'The caravan park is that way,' he said scathingly, pointing in the direction she had intended leaving the service station, 'not thisaway.' He jerked his thumb backwards.

That her destination wasn't the caravan park did not seem relevant at that moment.

'I—I'm sorry,' Jacqui muttered, hardly daring to look at the rear of her car. 'H-have I done any damage?'

'You bet you have! Good God, your rear bumper is locked over my front one! As if I wasn't late enough already.'

He was very close, and the menacing eyes that met hers were, she noticed, a very dark blue, with golden flecks glinting in them. Or maybe it was just the radiance from the setting sun.

Jacqui felt terrible. 'I really am sorry. I don't know what happened. . . I put it in first——'

'Like hell you did!' he fumed. 'A car in first doesn't hurtle backwards. When did you get your licence?' His stance was belligerent.

'Years ago,' she retorted, resenting his belittling manner. 'I'm sure I used the right gear. . .' Her eyes weren't quite on a level with his, but she was tall enough, she noted with satisfaction, not to have to look up to him. She was in the wrong, but he was over-reacting.

'I don't think there's any real damage,' she said, casting an eye over the locked bumpers. 'If we can get someone to lift my car off. . .' Again she met his gaze unwaveringly. 'I'll pay for the damage, if there is any, don't worry.'

'Where are you from?' he demanded.

'Melbourne.'

He snapped impatiently, 'Before that, I mean. You're a pom, aren't you?'

'Yes. . .from London,' she admitted reluctantly. It was no business of his.

'I thought so, from your accent. On holiday, I suppose.' He didn't wait for confirmation, but went on brusquely, 'Well, you'd better take a bit more care, or your trip's going to end in real disaster. If you don't know first gear from reverse and you get your directions all wrong. . .'

Jacqui bit her lip. She had no excuse, she deserved the tongue-lashing he was giving her, but did he need to be quite so abrasive? It was an accident, a careless action on her part, but it could happen to anyone. Besides, it was really his fault. Staring at her like that had confused her. She could hardly say that, however.

'You did park rather close behind me,' she defended.

He glared. 'There was ample room until you backed,' he said scathingly. He looked her up and down again. 'I suppose I ought to have known I should give a woman driver a wide berth.'

'I should certainly have given you one,' she snapped back, 'if I'd known how arrogant you were!'

He looked at her hard for a moment, while she braced herself for further sarcasm. It didn't eventuate. He said in a milder, but impatient tone, 'Well, I suppose I'd better get Lennie to prise us apart.' There was no twinkle of humour in the dark castigating eyes, suggesting a joke.

'I'm sorry it's holding you up.' Jacqui was feeling more helpless and inadequate with every second, as well as distinctly antagonistic towards the owner of the green car.

He was already walking away. Jacqui stared at the locked bumpers and wanted to burst into tears. What a start to her new life! Only the second local she'd encountered, she'd well and truly rubbed up the wrong way. Well, she'd been right about Akubra-hatted cowboys! They *were* arrogant and macho. Certainly this one was.

He came back with Lennie, who looked at the interlocked bumpers and grinned at Jacqui. 'Pity he didn't want a tow, eh?'

Jacqui bit her lip. The cowboy wasn't smiling either. Jokes were falling flatter than plates. 'Can you unhitch it?' He spoke in a much more friendly tone than he'd used with her.

'Yup,' said Lennie. 'Won't take a jiff. I'll just get the fork-lift.'

He loped off again and Jacqui was left in uncomfortable silence with the irate customer.

'I'm terribly sorry——' she began again.

He glanced at her. 'You're repeating yourself.'

Jacqui flinched. He had a quelling manner, this macho man. Having typed him as a grazier or farmer, she was glad she was a nurse and not some poor downtrodden jillaroo on his property. She only hoped he never let a tractor run over his foot, or was struck down by appendicitis and ended up in the hospital. Nursing a man like him would be a nightmare. You'd never be able to do a thing right, she suspected.

While they waited for Lennie, she continued to invent the worst character reference for him she could, even though the situation was probably making her exaggerate. He had every right to be angry, she reminded herself, and she had no right at all to resent it.

Lennie returned and within seconds had hooked up her bumper and disentangled the two cars. The cowboy backed his car out of the way. Inspection of the chrome revealed only minor scratches, much to Jacqui's relief.

She said, however, 'If you'll send me the bill——' But before she could tell him to send it to the hospital, not the caravan park, he butted in.

'Forget it. Just be thankful it wasn't worse. I'll let you off this time, but remember that next time you reverse instead of going forward you mightn't get let off so lightly. You might have a real accident.' He seemed to have calmed down now that the damage was revealed as very slight. In a less abrasive but not quite friendly tone, he said, 'Get along and pitch your tent or find your caravan before it gets dark. And while you're here, do try not to get into any real trouble. Our hospital is stretched enough without accident-prone tourists cluttering up its beds.'

The derision edging his tone nettled Jacqui anew, as did his assumption that she was just a pommy tourist, and the implication that as such she must be automatically irresponsible.

She drew herself up to her full five feet seven and gave him as piercing a glance as she could manage from her large brown eyes. 'I am *not* a *tourist*,' she said, emphasising the words.

He looked only mildly taken aback. 'What are you, then?' He evidently wasn't convinced.

'I'm the new charge nurse at Maneroo Hospital.' She was gratified by the look of astonishment that came into the cowboy's face.

Lennie, who had observed with interest, now said, 'She only just made it into town, didn't you, Sister? All she had left in the tank was a cupful.'

Jacqui could have slaughtered him for revealing that. The cowboy's expression registered derision again. 'Can one so careless as to run out of gas, put a car in reverse instead of first gear and get directions wrong really be a competent charge nurse?' he queried. 'What sort of mishaps can they expect at Lakeside, I wonder? Maybe I'd better warn them. . .'

'Go ahead,' Jacqui said wearily. 'I'm sure they'd appreciate it. I suspect, though, that they might be just a little bit more humanitarian than you, and understand that people do sometimes have a bad day! Perhaps you never make a mistake. You should have been a surgeon. The world doesn't know what it's missing.'

He took a long, cool look at her. Jacqui was aware of Lennie open-mouthed in the background, but she refused to be the first to look away. She wasn't going to be intimidated by this—this macho hayseed!

The shadows were lengthening and it was already dusk in the service station forecourt. 'Well, I'd better be getting along,' she said, and to the accompaniment of a wall of silence she got into her car and started the engine. As the two men turned away, she muttered, 'Arrogant cowboy!' then, carefully concentrating, she eased the car forward and with a feeling of relief left the service station. The last she saw of the cowboy, in her rear-vision mirror, was his lanky figure striding towards the garage shop with Lennie on the fork-lift. What was he late for? she wondered idly. A date with some submissive woman, no doubt.

'Well, I don't envy her,' she muttered, still fuming over the incident, while also feeling shamefaced, and with a return of her earlier apprehension. Supposing he did report the incident to the hospital? Would they be so unimpressed with her that they'd suggest she wasn't suitable for the job after all?

CHAPTER TWO

'WE'D expected you a little earlier,' Matron Wallace said over a small glass of sherry in her office, but she was not put out. She smiled. 'We were getting a little anxious, and hoping you hadn't lost your way.'

'The trip took longer than I'd thought,' Jacqui explained. 'I almost ran out of petrol and had to stop at the garage to fill up. I did go a bit wrong getting here, too. It was dark so suddenly.' There was no way she was going to relate her encounter with the cowboy at the service station.

'Never mind. You're here now, which is what matters. And I can tell you, we need you!' Matron showed visible relief, which made Jacqui feel that at least she was valued, even before she had proved herself. Matron went on, 'It's very hard to get good full-time nursing staff in the country. All the qualified nurses want to work in the city and get experience in the big hospitals.' She paused, flinty blue eyes that were not unkindly assessing Jacqui shrewdly.

'The agency told me I'd be filling in for a nurse who's on long service leave,' said Jacqui.

'That's right. Now, I'm sure you're anxious to settle into your quarters and get some rest.' She peered hopefully at Jacqui. 'Can you start tomorrow? We're very busy at the moment and short-staffed.'

'Yes, I can start tomorrow,' Jacqui said. She added, 'I understand I'm to share a house with three other nurses.'

Matron nodded. 'I'll get Jennie Morris to take you over as soon as you've had something to eat.'

Jacqui had a meal in the small staff canteen and met several of the nurses as well as one of the visiting medical officers, a GP in the town. There was a full-time MO, she was told, Dr David Darling. When she involuntarily smiled, Jennie, the nurse whom Matron had assigned to look after her, laughed.

'Terrible, isn't it? I don't know how he puts up with a name like that. Don't make any jokes about it! He goes spare if anyone does. It must have been murder for him at med school.' She flushed faintly. 'Actually he *is* a bit of a darling—fabulous-looking, and not married. I think he means to stay that way. He has quite a reputation around Maneroo for being the love-them-and-leave-them type. I don't know if he deserves it, but I do know he has all the nurses here eating out of his hand. . .anyway, you'll see for yourself when you meet him tomorrow.'

After the meal, Jennie took Jacqui on a brief tour of inspection, introducing her to a few more nurses, then escorted her to the house she would be sharing with her and two others.

'The part-timers all live locally,' Jennie told her, 'and most are married, which means we have a few problems with nurses being absent because their kids are sick. You can't just phone an agency to send an emergency nurse way out here, can you?'

By the time they reached the rambling old weather-board house in its spacious garden that was to be Jacqui's home for the next few months, or perhaps even longer if she liked it, Jacqui was yawning.

'You'd better get to bed,' Jennie advised. 'You look

as though you need a good sleep. What time are you
starting tomorrow?'

'I'm expected in by eight, I gather, but seven a.m.
after that.'

They entered the house, and Jennie shouted above
the strains of loud music from the living-room, 'Where
is everybody?'

The music faded and a head appeared with a towel
wrapped around it and vivid green face-mask disguising
its features.

'This is Elsa Graham, our physio,' said Jennie,
introducing Jacqui.

'Oh, hi,' said the green monster. 'Sorry about the
face pack. It's my answer to decadent living!'

'You'll see what she really looks like tomorrow,'
promised Jennie with a laugh. 'No improvement, as we
all keep telling her, but she doesn't believe it. Where's
Donna, Elsa?'

'Washing up, I guess. It was her turn tonight.'

Jacqui found herself propelled towards the kitchen
where she met Donna Mortlake, a rather more serious
girl with dark hair and startlingly blue eyes. She greeted
Jacqui in a friendly manner but with a certain reserve.

'Jacqui's ready to crash,' said Jennie, 'so I'll just
show her the flat and leave her to it.' To Jacqui, she
said, as they left, 'You being the senior staff member
get the flat—your own kitchen and bathroom and
separate entrance. You don't have to fraternise with us
if you don't want to, but you're welcome to drop in
any time. Just bang on the wall if Elsa has the music
up too loud.'

The flat was small but compact and comfortable. It
had been built on to the back of the house at some

time, probably before the house had been acquired to accommodate nurses.

Jacqui looked around with approval. 'It's very nice,' she commented. 'I feel favoured.'

Jennie said she'd better be getting back as there were a few things she had to do before she finished for the day and no one else would do them for her, that was for sure. She said cheerfully, 'Well, I'll let you get on with it. You'll find plenty of linen and the fridge and food cupboards stocked, but if you need anything, ask the girls.' She was about to leave when she hesitated. 'I guess I'd better warn you, keep your doors and windows locked at night, and don't wander around in the dark if you can help it. We've had a prowler problem for the last couple of months and until he's caught everyone's a bit edgy. Donna was attacked one night, just walking from the hospital to here. There's a short cut to the hospital through the back lane that joins the other end of this street, but only use it in broad daylight.' She bit her lip. 'I don't want to scare you, but I think you ought to know.'

'Thanks,' said Jacqui, 'I'll be careful.' Jennie was halfway through the door when she stopped her. 'Hey, you're not walking back there alone after what you've just told me!'

Jennie shrugged. 'Oh, he doesn't usually front up until later than this. It's probably safe enough this early in the evening. But I'll go the long way round anyway.'

'I'll drive you back,' Jacqui insisted. 'It won't take five minutes.'

Jennie did not argue. 'Thanks.'

Jacqui dropped her off at the hospital and then returned to her little flat with a definite lifting of spirits. It was luxury indeed to have such accommodation all to herself, and although she was dead tired she quickly penned a note to Lissa to thank her for Mopoke, whom she perched on a ledge above the bed, and to tell her briefly about her arrival. Excepting her fireworks with the cowboy. She didn't feel like dwelling on that, even to Lissa. She could still feel the tingling antagonism his manner had aroused, still see those piercing eyes dissecting her and finding the results unfavourable. He reminded her, she thought with a grim smile, of a certain senior house surgeon during her training who had seemed to regard it as his role in life to diminish every student nurse who crossed his path with either a crushing word or look. He'd also been devastatingly handsome and knew it. They'd called him Lucifer behind his back. Well, thank goodness she wasn't working for that antipodean Lucifer. A smile hovered over her lips for a moment. A blond Lucifer? It didn't really fit.

'Why am I even thinking about him?' she muttered. It was only because he'd made her feel a fool, and angry with herself for her own carelessness.

She was too tired to unpack her suitcases, so she left them standing in the living-room, extracting only what she needed for the night. She would be given a uniform, Matron had told her, when she reported for work in the morning. She was too tired even to make herself a hot drink. She simply undressed and fell into the already made up bed, and slept soundly until her alarm went off at a quarter to six.

As the weather was fine, Jacqui decided to explore the short cut to the hospital. She had no trouble finding the lane, and had progressed only a short distance along it when a bell heralded the approach of a bicycle which skidded to a halt alongside her.

'Hi!'

Jacqui glanced at the young woman questioningly.

The girl laughed. 'Elsa Graham! The green witch from last night, remember?'

'Oh, yes! Goodness, you do look different this morning. Much more appealing, I have to say.'

'You're on your way to the hospital?' Elsa enquired.

'Yes. It's such a lovely morning, I thought I'd walk.'

Elsa rode slowly alongside her. 'Don't do it at night if you can help it, though. We have a prowler.'

'Yes, Jennie told me about that.'

'He hasn't actually raped anyone yet, but until the police catch him we've been warned to be careful. He's a pretty elusive character—wears a stocking mask— and he's had the town on tenterhooks for a couple of months or more. It's possible he gets his kicks from just frightening women, but one can't be too careful.' Elsa gave a cheerful laugh. 'We ought to get danger money! Even on the wards you can get attacked. I remember a nurse who had scratches all down her face from some belligerent drunk who'd been in a road accident. She had scars for ages.'

'I've had a couple of close calls with violence myself,' Jacqui admitted, remembering several such occasions. 'Mostly in A and E departments, where violence seems to be most prevalent, but I'll never forget the ex-heavyweight boxer we had in once for surgery—a cholecystectomy, I think it was—and I found him wandering out of his room the night after his operation, trailing the drip and the stand and insisting on being discharged. Before help arrived, we night staff were dodging every punch in the book trying to get him back to bed. We laughed later, but it was scary at the time. He could have laid out any one of us. I suppose coping with violent patients is part of the job, but we can do without being harassed outside the hospital as well.'

When the lane ended, there was a path across the hospital grounds which joined the main driveway. In the car park, while Elsa tethered her bike in the rack, Jacqui paused to take in the view of lake and trees against the vivid blue sky. The air was clearer here, and sweeter smelling than in the city, where a haze seemed to blanket everything most of the time. She took a deep breath, and as she did so her eye alighted on a sleek green car facing out of one of the parking bays, most particularly on its front bumper.

'It's his!' she gasped aloud, suddenly filled with consternation. He must be in there now telling Matron Wallace what an incompetent fool the new charge nurse was, probably persuading her that Jacqui should not be trusted in charge of even a tea-trolley. She swallowed hard. She would have to face up to it. She just hoped Matron wasn't the kind to let one mishap override a clutch of excellent references.

'Did you say something?' Elsa rejoined her.

'No—no, I was just exclaiming at the view. I didn't really take it in last night. The hospital is certainly in a very pleasant setting. Good for convalescence.'

'Mmm,' agreed Elsa, as they walked up to the entrance. 'But I don't know for how much longer. There's a move afoot to close it down and send patients to the new hospital being built at Hindmarsh. Somebody has their eye on this valuable piece of real estate to develop it as a posh tourist resort. People are just beginning to discover the lake's potential for leisure activities and tourism is set to boom in Maneroo, so there's a fair bit of hard pressure being put on the town council, which owns the land.'

'But surely, with increased tourism, there'll be increased need for hospital facilities?' Jacqui suggested.

'The proposal is that we just retain a community health centre in Maneroo. Those in favour say people will prefer to go to the big new hospital anyway. It'll be only fifty or so kilometres away.'

'When will it be finished?'

'It's halfway to completion now, but there's been some industrial trouble and a shortage of funds, so work is held up. It'll be a few months yet before it opens.'

As they entered the building, Elsa said, 'Do you remember where Matron's office is?'

Jacqui nodded and they parted. The door to Matron's office was closed, but Jacqui could hear voices within, too muffled for her to distinguish whether they were male or female. She had the sinking feeling that the cowboy was in there now, assassinating her character. Well, what better time to defend herself? she thought, with a surge of defiance, and knocked lightly on the door.

'Come in!' Matron Wallace's strong voice commanded.

Jacqui pushed open the door. Bright light from the big window which faced into the early morning sun dazzled her for a moment, and she was aware only of a figure in blue, Mrs Wallace, and another in a white coat. 'Good morning,' Jacqui said tentatively.

'Ah, Jacqueline,' Mrs Wallace greeted her. 'Welcome again. Come on in and meet our resident MO. David, this is Jacqui Brent—taking Marion's place.'

'Actually,' drawled a horribly familiar voice, 'Sister Brent and I have already met.'

Mortified, Jacqui stared at the tall, rangy figure with

the wheat-blond hair and piercing dark blue eyes. The cowboy! He was Dr Darling. She felt as though she could have slid through a pin-hole in the floor if there had been one.

'You have?' Matron was querying in surprise. Then she chuckled. 'Trust you, David!'

'We were both filling our tanks at the service station last evening,' he explained, not taking his eyes from Jacqui, but letting them drift in leisurely fashion from her face to her feet and back again as though sizing her up for a strait-jacket. 'We had a short conversation then,' he murmured, and his mouth quirked a little. Jacqui decided not to assume it was a smile.

'That's the nice thing about small towns,' said Matron complacently. 'Everybody soon gets to know everybody else.' She glanced at her watch. 'If that's all, David, I'd better get Jacqui started. They're pretty hectic on Medical at the moment as you know, and although Angela's a very good nurse she's not an organiser.' She smiled at Jacqui. 'I hope you are!'

Jacqui caught Dr Darling's eye, which was nothing if not sardonic. She bristled inwardly. How dared he judge her on one small incident, one tiny error of judgement? And almost as if he'd spoken it, she heard in her head the salutary comment: one tiny error of judgement could cost a patient's life. She looked away from his piercing gaze and wondered if she would ever manage to redeem herself in the eyes of this uncompromising man. It was only professional pride, she told herself, as his white-coated figure went out, that made her want to.

There was one thing in his favour, however. Unless she was being ultra-diplomatic, Matron had not known they had met before, which meant that Dr Darling

could not have revealed the incident in the service
station and used it against her. She hugged that small
consolation to herself. Dr Darling might prove difficult
to get along with and a hard taskmaster, especially with
someone whose expertise he doubted, but it seemed as
though he was fair at least. He had not rushed to tell
tales on her. He must be prepared to give her a second
chance to prove her worth.

'And I will,' Jacqui muttered to herself in the
deserted nurses' room as she scrambled into the uniform provided. It was a colour that suited her red
hair—pale lilac. The material was a crisp cotton in a
very fine lilac and white stripe with white collar and
cuffs. It was the same as all the nurses wore, but with
the addition of a deeper toned cotton jacket, hip-length
and collarless, that designated her senior position.
Jacqui slipped into her white shoes and fastened the
velcro tabs. She pinned on her own clinical watch, then
set off for the medical ward where she was to take
over.

Matron was there talking to a nurse whose name,
Jacqui noticed from her security tag, was Angela.
Jacqui reminded herself not to forget to see Admin
about her own name-tag as soon as she had a chance.

Matron Wallace beamed at her. 'Jacqui, this is
Angela Forster, who'll show you the ropes.'

Angela held out her hand. 'Am I glad to see you,
Jacqui!'

Another pom, Jacqui noted as she shook hands with
the nurse and said, 'Hello. I gather you're pretty busy.'

Mrs Wallace said, 'I've got an appointment with the
hospital committee chairman, so I'll leave you girls to
carry on.'

As she left, Angela flipped a stray strand of blonde

hair behind her ear and said with a heartfelt sigh, 'Third time lucky! I don't suppose you know that we've had a charge nurse coming twice before and each one has pulled out at the last minute. I was getting desperate. I don't mind the nursing, but the paperwork, the rosters, the details. . .' She grinned. 'Oh, dear, don't let me put you off on your first day.'

'You're from where?' Jacqui queried.

'Near Basingstoke. You?'

'London. Wimbledon, to be precise.'

Angela laughed. 'With all of us poms taking over the Oz hospitals, I don't know how the NHS is managing to survive.'

'A lot go back,' said Jacqui. 'Some are disillusioned when it doesn't turn out quite the way they expect.'

Angela's green eyes twinkled. 'Or they don't snare a tall bronzed rich Aussie surgeon with a BMW or a Porsche!'

'How long have you been here?' asked Jacqui.

'Three years. Actually, I'm married to an Aussie GP. You'll meet him, he's a visiting MO here—Eric Forster.'

'You're happy here?'

'In Australia, you mean? Yes, very. I'm a country girl, so Maneroo suits me fine. Mind you, the big wide open spaces are a bit different from what I was used to, but, although I found it all rather empty and forbidding at first, I've got used to it. I wouldn't shift to the city for quids, which is just as well, because Eric's a country boy. His folks have a farm way out in the sticks. You'll find that Maneroo's a very friendly town, Jacqui. There's plenty of social activity, but the pace is easier——' Angela broke off and laughed. 'Not that you'd notice that in Lakeside at the moment.

We've a full house in Medical, and Surgical has a waiting list for tonsillectomies and other minor ops. When the new hospital's finished at Hindmarsh that might relieve the pressure, but meanwhile. . .' She picked up a pile of reports. 'Let's do a quick recce so you know what you've got in at the moment before David arrives to do his round—have you met David Darling, the resident MO, yet?' Jacqui nodded and Angela went on breezily, 'Darling by name, darling by nature, but don't imagine that means he's soft. He's a stickler for efficiency, can't stand untidiness, gossiping nurses, people standing around with nothing to do, and unpunctuality. He cracks down hard on newcomers and, when he's wiped the floor with them, he switches on the charm and seduces them with a look.'

'Sounds like Lucifer,' commented Jacqui.

'What?'

'A surgeon I used to loathe.'

'You won't loathe David, he's an absolute dish, but if he gives you an inch don't presume to take a yard. I might as well tell you he's reputedly a confirmed bachelor who adores women but abhors marriage. His words, apparently! His father's a retired GP in Maneroo and was a bit of a ladies' man himself in his youth, I've heard. Now, what I was going to say: David will appear at ten-thirty for routine ward rounds and afterwards he usually likes to spend a few minutes with you in the office discussing problems. If he isn't on hand at the time, he likes to see all new admissions promptly after admission whether their GPs have seen them or not.'

Angela raced on volubly, explaining the daily routine to Jacqui, who tried to take it all in and retain it. Almost at once she could see one or two administrative areas in which she could improve efficiency. Angela then took her to meet the patients and explain their conditions. There were two sections consisting of several rooms each, one for men, one for women patients, and a suitably decorated small four-bed ward for children. The nurses' station and charge nurse's office were in between, as were the nurses' lounge and kitchen, and ward facilities.

'I'll come with you if you like when David does his round,' Angela offered. She grinned. 'For moral support!'

Dr David Darling appeared at exactly ten-thirty. Jacqui was alone in the office, reading through case histories, as Angela had gone off to help one of the other nurses adjust a drip for the recently admitted peptic ulcer patient as it had not been functioning properly.

'Good morning again, Sister Brent.'

Jacqui had been so absorbed she had not heard the door open. The sound of his voice jerked her head up. 'Dr Darling. . .er, yes, good morning, again.' She stood up hastily. 'I—er—Angela's helping one of the others adjust a drip for Mr Ferguson. . .'

He said nothing for a moment, then rapped out, 'Shouldn't you be supervising?'

Jacqui was taken aback. 'I'm sure Angela is quite capable. . .after all, until this morning she's been in charge here.'

He eased his large frame into the room. He looked different in his white coat, and she kept thinking of him in the cowboy gear. The slim hips and muscular thighs were now concealed, as was the fringe of tawny hair that had shown in the V of his open-neck shirt. He didn't look quite so earthy now in a roll-neck grey skivvy and grey trousers under the unbuttoned white coat, but just as formidable. Angela was wrong. She probably was going to loathe this blond Lucifer.

'You're in charge now,' he said, following that remark with, 'Shall we go and check it out?'

Jacqui fervently wished she had gone with Angela as it had been her first instinct to do, but she had not been asked to, and on this her first day she had thought it best not to throw her weight around too much. She didn't want Angela to resent her. She'd decided to keep as low a profile as possible for a few days until she had setled in and was accepted. But Dr Darling was evidently not going to let her do things her way.

'Certainly,' she answered. 'If you're ready to do your round now, I am.'

His eyes skated across her face, a critical glance. He said, 'I'm glad to see you adopt a sensible hairstyle for work.'

Jacqui felt her skin prickle with annoyance at his tone, but she forbore to say anything. They went out, he holding the door for her, and standing so that she had difficulty going through without brushing against him. She caught a faint whiff of spicy aftershave and her cheek tingled as his warm breath brushed it fleetingly.

They went first to Mr Ferguson's room. Angela and another nurse were still fiddling with the drip. Both looked round as Jacqui and David Darling entered.

Angela looked flustered. 'We're having a problem with the drip, David. I thought it just needed an adjustment to the angle of the tube. . .'

He strode across to the equipment. Jacqui glanced at the patient, who seemed to be asleep and unaware of the fuss going on around him. In seconds, Dr Darling had adjusted the drip, checked the infusion site in the man's hand, and the patient's pulse and general condition.

'He's been giving that stomach of his a hard time for too many years,' he remarked, as they went out. 'And I don't think his liver's going to stand it much longer either. He collapses in the local park or outside the pub and ends up here, about every six months. Lately it's been more like every three.'

'There's not a lot you can do about alcoholism unless the will to give it up is there,' said Jacqui, saddened by the sight of the man, who was only fifty but looked much older.

Dr Darling glanced at her. There was anger in his face, but not for her. 'He had a wife and kids once, but he used to bash them up when he was drunk, so finally they left him. No, there isn't much you can do. We dry him out, settle his ulcer, then turn him out until the next time.'

The scene was a little more cheerful in the next room, which was shared by three male patients. One was a rather gaunt man who had been admitted with ulcerative colitis. He was due to be discharged.

'You'll need to watch your diet, Joe,' Dr Darling told him, 'and go easy on the booze in particular.'

'I might fancy being readmitted,' said Joe with a grin at Jacqui. 'The nurses are getting prettier every day.'

'That's because you're getting older every day,' said David.

He worked methodically from bed to bed, room to room, not wasting a minute, yet giving the impression, Jacqui thought, that he had all the time in the world to stop and chat. He got more than a few admiring looks from the women patients, she noticed.

For her, it was all rather a strain. She was grateful for Angela's familiarisation tour that morning, as that prior knowledge saved her on more than one occasion. Dr Darling was fond of asking snap questions and expecting an instant answer. His intimidating blue gaze was enough to faze anyone, but she suspected he was testing her and was not usually so sharp.

At the end of the round, her tension relaxed, but the relief was premature. David Darling strolled back with her to her office and sprawled in a chair as though he'd come to stay.

'There are a few things I'd like to talk to you about,' he said. 'How about asking someone to bring us coffee?'

Jacqui was feeling drained and would have preferred some time to herself, but she was obliged to say, 'All right. . .'

Everyone was busy, so she made it herself and carried two mugs back to the office. His fingers touched hers as she handed him his mug and she wished she'd just placed it on the desk instead. He regarded her steadily, then launched into details of a new routine he wanted instituted for admissions and discharges. Jacqui listened carefully and made notes. What she didn't say was that she had been thinking along similar lines ever since Angela had outlined the current procedure. But she didn't tell David Darling that.

He made one caustic remark. 'I hope you've got those instructions the right way round,' he said, after firing a barrage of them at her. 'You'd better read them back to me.'

Jacqui flinched at the reminder of her slip in remembering the directions she'd been given at the service station, but kept calm and said, 'Certainly.' To her relief, she had got down everything he had said correctly.

Finally he stood up to go. He stood for a moment looking down at her then, hands on the desk, leaning towards her, he said, 'You don't have to wear a hair shirt forever because you bashed my bumper yesterday. I've quite forgiven you!'

Jacqui felt her face flame. She remembered what Angela had said about him wiping the floor with people, then turning on the charm. He'd successfully reduced her to a quivering wreck, and now was forgiving her! What was so maddening was that she'd let him do it. She, a mature twenty-five-year-old experienced senior nurse, had let herself be intimidated by an arrogant so-and-so of a doctor as though she were a first-year.

'So what am I supposed to do now?' she demanded, going to the opposite extreme. 'Go down on bended knee and say thank you very much?'

A low, throaty chuckle reverberated round the room. 'I can tell that red hair is the real thing! We shall have to watch our step around here.' He angled his head slightly and observed her critically. 'Actually, your hair looks much more attractive tumbling about your face.'

While Jacqui gazed open-mouthed and speechless after him, he turned and strode out of the room.

CHAPTER THREE

As HE had surprised himself doing many times recently, David Darling stood at the window of his office watching Lakeside's new charge nurse, Jacqui Brent, strolling down to the lake. In her hand was the brown paper bag containing her lunch sandwiches, half of which would be cadged from her by the black swans which had seen her and were already heading shorewards. Not for the first time, he experienced a strong urge to follow her, to talk to her not as a nurse but as a person with another life, another dimension.

It was three weeks since Jacqui had arrived, and his lips curved in a reminiscent smile as he recalled their first prickly encounter. She seemed to have forgiven his abrasiveness that night, but perhaps had not forgotten. Of course he hadn't told her why he'd been in such a foul mood. She kept a cool distance between them, a polite professional barrier that he found daunting. Any other woman as attractive as Jacqui Brent would have been on his dating list long ago. It wasn't as though she'd rebuffed him. He simply hadn't plucked up the courage to ask her out yet. At least that was what he told himself, because a cautionary inner voice suggested that a relationship with Jacqui Brent, if started, might be a hard one to break. He didn't want to get involved. One mistake was enough. There were fewer hassles in freedom, and there were enough responsibilities in his professional life at the hospital without filling his free time with more.

He watched her tall, slim figure walk gracefully towards the water's edge where there were benches. A nurse wheeling a patient in a wheelchair approached, and Jacqui paused to talk to them. He felt a strong resentment because she was so cool and clinical with him, yet open and friendly with everyone else.

She was popular with the patients and the staff. She had reorganised Medical in a week and the confusion that had sometimes maddened him since her predecessor had left had vanished in a matter of days. It was rare nowadays for him to find fault with the running of Lakeside's medical ward.

He watched her throw back her head and laugh, then clamp a hand on the patient's shoulder in a reassuring manner as she bent towards him to say something. Her red hair gleamed in the sunlight. It was coiled as usual into a chignon, pulled back from her calm oval face, but as usual, he guessed, there would be rebellious curls escaping the pins to give a softer frame to her features. It was hard sometimes to resist the urge to tear out all those restraining pins and let the rich coppery tresses fall to her shoulders, the way he'd first seen them, giving the smooth peach-bloom skin a warmer glow.

There was an almost imperceptible sprinkling of freckles on her cheekbones and the tip of her slightly tip-tilted nose. Her mouth always seemed to be on the brink of smiling, yet she seldom smiled at him. She always seemed ill at ease in his company, as though waiting for him to pounce on some shortcoming. She was unflappable, yet her conscientiousness made her sensitive. He'd started off on the wrong foot with her, so they'd probably never reach a really warm accord.

Did that matter? Hadn't he told himself he didn't want to get involved with her?

Nevertheless she intrigued him, and his masculine impulses indicated that he wanted very much to date her, have fun with her, run his fingers through that glorious hair, let them encircle that slender waist. He didn't mind that he wouldn't have to bend his head to kiss her because her lips were nearly on a level with his. He liked tall girls, and he especially liked the way she always looked him straight in the eye. He liked her soft English accent, the slightly hesitant way she called him David as though fearing she was being too familiar.

He turned angrily away from the window. 'Damn it!' he muttered. 'Damn the woman!' He threw himself into his desk chair and stared at the stack of paperwork before him. He was not going to let the red-haired pommy nurse get under his skin. *Definitely not.*

Jacqui sat down on her usual bench and smiled at the convoy of swans approaching the bank. The black ducks from which Lake Maneroo got its Aboriginal name were converging too. The birds had quickly become used to her regular lunchtime visits and the crusts she threw to them. Usually there were one or two convalescing patients down there too, but today there was no one else on the lakeside walk. She was one of the few staff who went out at lunchtime, but she'd got into the habit early on and enjoyed the break in the fresh air and sun. Cutting her own sandwiches was a new habit too. Lakeside was changing her, she sometimes thought, only half jokingly.

In three weeks she had settled down remarkably well. Melbourne seemed almost as far away as England, and the hurt and humiliation that Carey had inflicted, which she had expected to stay with her for a long time, was already fading. Her misgivings about taking the country job had almost disappeared.

I couldn't have been in love with Carey, she had decided recently. It was his charm, the glamorous, hectic pace of his life, that attracted me. I should have seen that there was no substance to it. I was a gullible fool. I was lucky to escape when I did. Without even a broken heart, she eventually admitted, astonished. One thing she was sure of, and that was that she was never going to be fooled by a man again. She was too much like her own mother, too trusting, too ready to take people at face-value, which made her a bad judge of character. If she ever fell in love again it was going to be with someone plain and ordinary and totally without charisma. She was never going to let a man sweep her off her feet again.

There was only one small blight on her contentment with Lakeside, and that was Dr Darling. She could never feel at ease with him. She had already come to admire him and respect his medical knowledge and decisiveness, his cool analytical mind, his warm manner with the patients, but about the person behind the professional mask she knew nothing. He was outwardly friendly towards her now, but there remained a barrier between them because of that first unfortunate encounter. She still felt he had reservations about her competence, and, despite herself, she was always on tenterhooks when he was around, as though expecting him to find fault. He rarely did, but it didn't seem to make any difference. After his apology, or rather his condescension in forgiving her, she had half expected him to follow up according to the pattern Angela had warned her about and ask her out, but he hadn't. Perhaps he sensed that she would have rebuffed him.

There was no way she would begin even the most casual personal relationship with David Darling. He had far too much charisma.

Nevertheless, it occasionally teased her mind, as on most days when she was alone, eating her sandwiches at the lakeside, to imagine how a date with David would be.

The glossy black swans stood in a semicircle watching her expectantly, snapping their crimson beaks and fidgeting their webbed feet. Jacqui threw her crusts to them. One really tame bird came close and she fed him from her hand. A crowd of seagulls swooped in, and a few sparrows pecked around her feet. The lake lapped gently against the stone edging and Jacqui felt, as usual, at peace.

'I'm very happy here,' she had written to Lissa recently. And it was true. So far, she had felt no sudden yearning for city life, and that despite not yet having involved herself in any local social activities apart from a visit to the cinema with a couple of other nurses. She had been invited to join the tennis club, however, to give a lecture on mouth-to-mouth resuscitation at the youth club, and to a birthday party on Saturday at one of the nurses' homes. Her mind had switched to wondering what she should wear to the party when a voice startled her.

'Mind if I join you?'

His shoes had made no sound on the grass as he approached from behind. Jacqui turned round.

'David! No, of course not.' She glanced at the plastic-wrapped sandwiches from the canteen and the carton of coffee he was carrying.

'It was such a nice day I thought I'd eat out,' he told her, taking the far end of the bench and setting his lunch on it between them. 'I see you had the same idea.'

'Yes, I often eat my sandwiches down here,' Jacqui said.

He didn't let on that he knew that. He was still wondering at the motivation that had sent him speeding to the canteen and hotfooting it across the grass to the lakeside before her lunchbreak ended. He grinned at her. 'Your—er—friends won't mind?' He didn't feel exactly welcomed, either by her or the swans, one of whom was hissing softly at him.

Jacqui recovered her composure. 'I think they're as surprised as I am. You don't usually dine al fresco, do you?'

'No, but it occurs to me I ought to do it more often.' Her slight frown made him add to avoid misunderstanding, 'Fresh air and a little exercise is what we recommend for the patients' good health, so why not for our own? You've got the right idea.'

Who did he think he was kidding? Jacqui thought, then changed her mind. If he really wanted to chat her up, this was an odd time to pick. How did he know she was here anyway? Maybe she ought to believe it was merely coincidence.

'You've settled in well,' David ventured, tearing crusts off his bread for the swans. 'But you're missing city life, I suppose.'

'Not really.'

He said drily, 'You city slickers don't usually last long. You'll soon get tired of country living.' There was a derogatory note in his voice, but he softened it with a faint smile. He hadn't meant to be arch with her.

Jacqui ignored the barb. 'It makes a pleasant change

to work in a smaller hospital. I've always nursed in larger ones.'

'What made you decide to change?'

The truth was not for his ears. 'Curiosity, spirit of adventure. Bit of both.' She gave him an ironic look. 'And of course a tourist's desire to see more of the country.'

He laughed at the reminder of their first encounter. 'Working holiday, is it? A few months here and there to pay for the sightseeing. Nursing's a good way to see the world.'

'It hasn't been quite like that so far. I've only had a couple of very brief holidays.'

'You were at South City General before you came here, I gather?'

She asked cautiously, 'Do you know people there?'

He nodded. 'I did my internship at the SCG. Great hospital. Where did you work in London?'

'The Central.'

'I spent two years at St Thomas's. A mate of mine was at the Central.'

'Most of the Australian doctors and nurses I've met seem to have spent some time working in London,' Jacqui remarked.

'It's almost obligatory, from a social if not a professional standpoint.'

'But you came back here?'

'Eventually.' His features darkened for a moment and Jacqui sensed that some painful experience might have influenced him. 'The Darlings have been ministering to the inhabitants of Maneroo and district for several generations. My father's retired now. He and my mother are away on a trip to Europe at the moment.'

There was a silence during which they both contemplated the birds who were still fussing around hopefully. Finally, Jacqui asked, 'What will happen to the staff when Lakeside closes? Will they be offered posts in the new hospital?'

He gave her the sort of look that suggested she'd mixed up prescriptions. 'Lakeside's closure is not a *fait accompli*. The Government might want to close it down, but locally there's quite a lot of support for keeping it, even enlarging it.'

'I thought the local council was keen to sell the land to a developer for a tourist complex,' Jacqui said.

'Over my dead body!'

Her eyebrows rose. 'But won't you be a candidate for one of the consultant positions at the new hospital?'

'You've been listening to gossip,' he reproached her.

He didn't elaborate, but threw his last crust to a demanding swan almost at his knee and switched the conversation back to her. 'You know, when you arrived, I had the feeling you were a bit distraught.' He eyed her steadily. 'I thought maybe you were running away from something—or someone. . .?' It was a daring question, but it had been plaguing him. She'd been in a highly strung state that evening she'd backed into his car, and he'd realised it afterwards. Later he'd formed the impression that there was something secretive about her, some wall to break through, before he would really get to know her. Her aloofness with him had to be because of a man, he'd thought, and the way she stiffened now confirmed it.

'I don't know what gave you that idea.'

'Women as attractive as you usually have men in their lives.'

'In their *private* lives,' she said, with a look that told

him to mind his own business, but which further supported his feeling that flight to Maneroo had been for deeply personal reasons, not the superficial ones she'd given.

Jacqui glanced at her watch. 'I'd better be getting back.' She rose, then said, 'If you've got time this afternoon, I'd like to talk to you about Mr Godfrey.' The patient was an elderly farmer who had suffered a cerebral haemorrhage a few weeks ago. He had lost the use of his left side and his speech was affected. Jacqui was worried about his rehabilitation when he left hospital.

'Old Wilf? I'll walk back with you and you can tell me now,' David invited, getting up. He dropped his crushed paper cup and sandwich wrap into the bin and caught up with her as she headed for the pathway back to the hospital. 'What's the problem?'

'It's his home situation. I don't think he's going to get the encouragement to improve that he should. And, despite his age, I think he's got a good chance of regaining some use of his limbs and improving his speech.' She paused, fearing she'd expressed an opinion she wasn't really qualified to.

David merely said, 'He's down for physiotherapy sessions twice weekly and speech therapy, isn't he?'

'Yes, but I sense that Mrs Godfrey doesn't have much faith in such treatment. As she plainly put it to me, "A stroke's a stroke, dear, and you have to learn to live with it." Mrs G nursed her mother after a severe stroke and now feels she knows all there is to know about brain damage.'

'We can't force people to accept treatment.'

'No, but in this case we might be able to push things in the right direction. The Godfreys' daughter came to see me the other day after she'd visited her father. She lives in Maneroo, runs a babies' and children's wear shop, and she wants to have her parents to live with her for a few months, or at least her father if Mrs G won't leave the farm, so he's handy for rehab treatment. At the moment Mrs G won't hear of it, insists he'll be better off on the farm, which his son is running, I gather, and that she'll drive him in to his appointments. She's over seventy and Joanna's afraid there'll be a lot of missed appointments for all sorts of reasons, and I'm inclined to agree with her.'

'Have you talked to Mrs Godfrey about it?'

'Yes, but she's adamant. The trouble is she doesn't understand what tremendous improvements have been made in rehabilitating stroke sufferers since she nursed her mother thirty years ago. I thought maybe you could persuade her.' Jacqui smiled at him. 'Pull something out of the hat!'

He groaned. 'I know Mrs Godfrey, and you're asking the impossible. If she's hell-bent on self-imposed martyrdom, nothing will budge her. Poor old Wilf. . .'

'You will try?'

He turned to look at her. 'You get involved, don't you?'

She felt it was an implied criticism. 'Do you agree he ought to stay with his daughter for a while?' she asked stiffly.

He didn't answer. They had reached the entrance and he held the door open for Jacqui. In the wind, more strands than usual had escaped her chignon and his fingers itched to smooth the shining curls into place.

'Tell Mrs Godfrey I want to have a word with her next time she visits,' he said, and Jacqui, who had felt rebuffed, gave him such a grateful smile that it haunted him for the rest of the day.

She found herself thinking over their lunchtime conversation several times during the rest of the day, despite the fact that she was busy. It had been a strange interlude. They hadn't really come any closer on a personal level, but at least she'd talked to him about the Godfreys and she felt sure he'd do something if he could. Mr Godfrey would be going home next week.

On Friday, just as she was tidying up, ready to leave, there was a crisis. An asthmatic child was rushed in, seriously ill, and for half an hour there was a touch-and-go situation.

Jacqui's heart missed a beat when she saw the grey pallor, the 'fishy' eyes of the young boy struggling to breathe. The awful wheezing was all too familiar. 'He's beginning to look cyanosed,' she murmured anxiously, as she and Jennie eased the boy on to the bed while another nurse banked up the pillows. Within moments, Dr Darling was on the scene.

He burst into the ward almost right behind the orderlies who had brought the patient straight from A and E to the intensive care ward where he was immediately connected to a respirator.

'Who brought him in? A parent?' David demanded.

Jacqui answered. 'Mother. She's just outside.'

'Find out what anti-spasmodic he's been using and how often. I don't want to give him a lethal dose.' Fingers on the boy's pulse, he met her eyes. 'And hurry. I don't like the look of this one.'

Jacqui flew. She knew that severe asthma attacks, especially prolonged ones, could lead to sudden death, especially in children. Within moments she had extracted details of the medication the boy had been having from his distraught mother, as well as the information that he'd had several attacks recently and that this one had been going on for some hours already. She consulted David and then sped to get the adrenalin injection he requested.

'I'll give him this now,' David said, taking the syringe from her, 'and see how he responds. If it isn't satisfactory, we'll set up an aminophylline IV. Meanwhile, keep up the oxygen therapy, and I want his condition monitored continuously.' With a look that brooked no argument, he added, 'I'd prefer you to special this patient, Jacqui.'

It was tantamount to a compliment. It meant that he trusted her more than anyone else. She nodded. 'All right, I'll stay.'

He brushed her hand with his. 'Good girl. The next few hours will be crucial.' Then, when he was satisfied that the boy's condition was under control for the time being, he said, 'Obs every ten minutes, please. I'll go and talk to his mother.'

Jacqui took up her position at the boy's bedside and watched with a small prayer in her heart for the young life struggling to survive. She kept her eagle eye on him, as well as taking his pulse and blood-pressure readings. The observant human eye, she knew only too well, could note significant small changes in the condition of a critical patient often more accurately than even modern technology. Robots would never replace nurses, one of her instructors had said in all seriousness.

After he had spoken to the boy's mother, David ushered her into the ward, gently explained what treatment her son was having and reassured her.

'It's a severe attack,' he told her honestly, 'but we have it under control now. Malcolm's a healthy child and not in any immediate danger. Sister Brent will stay with him and if there's any problem she'll call me at once. If you want to stay too, that's all right.' His voice was calm, reassuring the distraught mother, and Jacqui saw her visibly relax.

David departed, but it seemed he was never far away. Every few minutes he was back to check on progress, and each time he paused for further reassuring words to Malcolm's mother.

'He's breathing much easier now, Mrs Garland. But he's going to be very exhausted after such a prolonged bout.'

Talking to Mrs Garland herself, Jacqui learned that she was a widow, struggling to bring up three children alone. Her husband had been killed in a road accident two years before, and since then Malcolm's asthma attacks had worsened.

'But never as bad as this,' she said, still in a distraught tone. 'It terrified me. It was like he was suffocating. The spinhaler was no use at all.'

'It's terrifying for the victim too,' said Jacqui, 'and panic, of course, makes it even worse. You got him here just in time, Mrs Garland.'

Malcolm's mother began weeping quietly, her tension finally finding complete release. Jacqui let her cry for a few moments, knowing that tears would ease her anxiety a little. Then she pressed the bell and asked for a cup of tea for her and a more comfortable chair. Mrs Garland was going to have a long vigil. Jacqui knew she would not want to leave her son's bedside until she was absolutely sure he was going to be all right. In a comfortable chair she might at least doze off without realising it.

It was well into the night when David insisted that Jacqui be relieved. He spoke to her outside the ward. 'You've had a long day,' he said. 'You've got a full complement on the night shift, so you can go home now. The worst is over, I think.' He added with cautious confidence, 'He's responding well. I'm a bit concerned about acidosis, but we'll fix that with an IV. Has he taken any fluids by mouth?'

'A few sips of water.'

He nodded. 'I'm afraid Malcolm could prove to be a case of status asthmaticus. The family situation is pretty tense, I gather, and that could be contributing, leading to over-use of anti-spasmodics which can be more dangerous than the asthma.'

Jacqui enlightened him further. 'It seems his mother has a boyfriend and Malcolm doesn't like him. He threw a tantrum yesterday, which might have been the trigger for this attack.'

'Is the boyfriend looking after the other children?'

'Apparently.'

David gave a faint smile. 'He can't be too bad!'

Jacqui, to her embarrassment, couldn't quite stifle a yawn. She felt bone-weary. A crisis right at the end of what had already been a hectic day had taken its toll of her both physically and emotionally.

David spread a large hand on her shoulder. 'You've had it—it's time you went home. We'll talk about after-care another time. No hurry. That young man is going to stay in for a few days at least.'

'You—you can call me if I'm needed,' she said, feeling that she was somehow deserting.

'I think we can manage,' he said with a smile. 'Now

run along and get your beauty sleep.' Warm blue eyes lingered on her tired ones and he murmured, 'Not that you need it for that.' Daringly, he lifted a corkscrew strand of hair and curled it behind her ear.

Jacqui drew back involuntarily, shocked by the sensation that ran through her at a mere touch of warm fingers on her temple. Every pulse in her body raced. David dropped his hand as though caught disobeying a 'Don't touch' notice on fragile porcelain.

A few moments later, he looked into her office where she was just tidying up, alone. 'I've just remembered—you walk to work, don't you?'

'Yes.' She was surprised he'd noticed.

'I'll drive you home.'

'No, really, it's all right.'

He merely said, 'Come on.'

Jacqui obediently followed him, but halfway along the corridor, his bleeper sounded. 'Hang on a minute,' he said briskly. 'I'll just see what the problem is. If I can't drive you, I'll get someone else to. Wait in the foyer.'

He was away in a flurry of coat-tails, leaving her somewhat bemused to continue on to the hospital entrance. When ten minutes later he hadn't returned, she decided not to wait any longer. He'd probably forgotten her. She asked the receptionist on duty to tell him she'd gone, in case he did come back.

Jacqui had always finished before dark and walked home in the light. She was pleased to see that there was a moon tonight. She set off through the car park and down the long poplar-lined driveway towards the entrance gates at a brisk pace. The path leading to the back lane branched off about two thirds of the way along. Her mind was still churning with the events of the past few hours and she longed for morning when she would know if Malcolm Garland had pulled through. The next few hours could be as crucial as the last few, she knew very well, despite David's optimism.

She was still some distance from the turn-off leading to the back lane when she thought she saw a movement in the shadows beyond the poplars lining the driveway. A slight shiver of apprehension ran through her as she stared hard into the island shrubberies that turned this part of the grounds into a kind of woodland. She saw nothing and decided she must have imagined it. Clouds crossing the moon were making the shadows seem to move. She kept on walking briskly, her feet crunching on the gravel echoing more loudly, it seemed now. The low drive-lights gave only enough illumination to guide motorists, and were no comfort. A few paces further on she was sure she glimpsed a movement again. There was no cloud crossing the moon. Was someone keeping pace with her beyond the trees?

Fright took a stranglehold on her throat for a moment, and she swallowed hard. She was vulnerable, walking alone along this deserted driveway, and once on the unlighted pathway she would be even more so. She was so used to walking home that even though it was dark she had not given a thought to prowlers. Besides, there had been no incidents since she'd come to Lakeside.

She glanced over her shoulder. The lights of the hospital seemed distant but looked infinitely more safe than the gloom ahead. Even walking the long way round, she was still vulnerable if someone was stalking her. Reacting to a surge of panic, Jacqui turned and fled back the way she had come. When headlights dazzled her she almost collapsed with relief. A car was coming. Frantically she flagged it down.

'Jacqui. . .Good God. . .'

David was out of the car, holding her trembling body tightly. Jacqui clung to him in relief, unable to speak for a moment. Then she gulped and said raggedly, 'The prowler. . .he was following me. . .' She was conscious suddenly of the strength and security of David's arms around her, and the urge to bury her face in his jacket and cling to him was strong.

David said grimly, 'Why didn't you wait for me? You know it could be dangerous to walk home alone in the dark.'

'I—I didn't want to bother you. . .'

The blue eyes were penetrating, censorious. 'I couldn't believe you'd gone. Maria on the front desk said you'd left only a minute ago, so I hoped to catch you. I couldn't believe my eyes when I saw you pelting back towards me.'

'I feel a bit of a fool,' Jacqui said, still shaking. 'There probably wasn't anyone there at all. It could have been just my imagination.'

'Don't talk like that—even if it's true. There has been a prowler, so we can't be too careful. Look, I'll take you home and we'll ring the police. Not that they'll catch him now. He won't have hung around, you can be sure, but we should report it anyway.'

'I feel as though I'm making a fuss about nothing. . .'

'Nonsense. It's a very serious matter.' He looked into her face with grave concern. 'You're not the type to run from shadows, or panic without good reason. It's my bet that your prowler was very substantial indeed. Come on, get in.'

With one arm firmly around her, he guided her

round to the passenger door and opened it. Jacqui almost collapsed into the seat. She wished her hands would stop shaking. She clasped them together tightly in her lap to control the trembling.

In less than five minutes, David was parked outside the house and she was unlocking the front door. The rest of the house was in darkness. Elsa and Donna must be on night duty as well as Jennie.

'You need a warm drink,' said David, and made straight for the kitchen.

He's been here before, Jacqui thought, and wondered if he and her predecessor, Marion, who had also lived in the flat, had been romantically involved. She followed him slowly. Tiredness had drained her and her flight had used up all her adrenalin. She flopped on to a chair and bowed her head on to her folded arms. While the kettle was boiling, David went to the phone and she heard him giving details to the police.

A few moments later he placed a mug of warm milky coffee on the table beside her and roused her. 'Here, drink this. It'll help to relax you and get your blood sugar moving again.' He smiled at her wan face. 'You sure can run, lady! That was a three-minute mile you were set on doing.'

Jacqui laughed and gulped the hot drink gratefully. The warmth coursed through her until her fingers and toes tingled and life came back into her body. David perched on the table edge and watched. A spurt of anger ran through him. If anything had happened to her. . .

'You're looking very fierce,' she told him. 'You must be angry with me after all. I do feel a fool——'

He leaned forward and thumped his fist on the table. 'I'm not angry with *you*! I'm angry with that sex maniac out there who goes around scaring the wits out of women. Why don't the damn cops get him?'

'I expect they will, eventually.' She stared into her drink.

'But maybe not before someone gets. . .'

'. . .raped,' she finished for him. She looked up. 'It's one of the hazards women face, David. One of the problems in our society that seems to be getting worse, and no one knows what to do about it. The law is still too lenient.'

He crashed his fist into his palm. 'You're damn right about that. I know what I'd do.'

'Why don't you make yourself a cup of coffee?'

He leapt up. 'I did!' He turned and grabbed it off the counter, where Jacqui had not noticed it. He pulled out a chair now and sat down opposite her. 'Feeling better?'

'Yes, thanks.' She blurted, 'Was I glad to see your headlights!'

'Am I glad I came after you!'

Eyes met and they exchanged a rueful smile. Jacqui felt a yawn rising in her throat. 'I—I'm sorry,' she murmured as it escaped.

'Maybe you're relaxed enough to sleep now,' said David. He drained his mug. 'I don't like leaving you alone. . .'

'Oh, really! I'm quite all right, David. There's no need to fuss. I always lock my doors and windows at night, except the bedroom, which has a grille on it. I'm a bit shaken, but I'm not scared of being alone. I feel more embarrassed than nervous.'

'Well, if you're quite sure. . .'

Jacqui appreciated his concern. 'You'd better be

getting back,' she said, getting up. 'Thanks for bringing me home. I'm quite all right now, truly.'

'I'll make sure there's an alert out to all nursing staff tomorrow,' he said as she accompanied him to the door. 'Never mind if it's a false alarm. People become too complacent when nothing happens for a while. It's better to be safe than sorry. Promise me you'll never walk home in the dark again, alone.'

'Yes. It was pretty stupid of me not to wait,' she answered soberly, holding the door open for him. 'Thanks again, David.'

He seemed about to bolt through, but suddenly paused, turned to her again, and, with what seemed an impulsive gesture, slid his hands into her hair until the pins scattered on the floor and it tumbled about her face in disarray.

'Hey, what are you doing?' She was half laughing, half dismayed.

'I just wanted to see you the way you were the first time I saw you,' he murmured, taking a long look at her face in the mellow glow from the hall lamp. He leaned forward and brushed his lips lightly across hers. 'Goodnight, Jacqui. Take care.' And then he was gone.

Jacqui closed the door, locked it and put the chain on. She stood for a moment with her knuckles pressed against her lips, trembling now for a very different reason.

CHAPTER FOUR

DESPITE her unnerving experience the previous night, Jacqui slept well. Her weariness and the warm drink David had made for her had overcome any lingering nervousness that might have encouraged insomnia. She was awake early as usual, but languished for a time, going over it all in her mind. She was almost convinced now that she had imagined the prowler, and felt rather shamefaced about it. She was glad she was off duty for the weekend, so avoiding any fuss at the hospital.

She had just finished breakfast when the police arrived. As they questioned her thoroughly, she felt more and more of a fraud, finally telling them so. The senior constable, however, shook his head and said more or less the same as David had.

'You don't seem like the sort to jump at shadows. He's been lying low for a few weeks, but that's the way these guys operate. Don't play it down, Sister. It's a serious matter.'

After they'd left, Jacqui went to the phone, anxious to reassure herself about Malcolm. Li Nguyen was on duty in her place this morning.

'Oh, hello, Jacqui,' said Li. 'How are you? We heard you had a lucky escape from the prowler last night.'

'I didn't actually see him,' Jacqui told her, 'but it was a bit unnerving at the time. I was sure someone was stalking me in the trees along the driveway. I'm fine now, though.'

'I wish they would catch that prowler,' Li said. 'He's got everyone on edge.'

Not wanting to dwell on her foolhardiness in walking home in the dark, Jacqui rushed on quickly, 'Li, how's the asthmatic boy?'

'Malcolm Garland? He's OK, Jacqui. He had a little cereal and a warm drink this morning. He's pretty washed out, but David's satisfied his condition has stabilised. We've still got him in the oxygen tent. His mother's looking a whole lot happier too. She's just gone home, but she'll be back later on.' Li paused, then said, 'I just saw David go past. Do you want to have a word with him?'

'No. . .no, don't bother him. I just wanted to find out how Malcolm was, that's all. Thanks, Li. I'm so glad he's OK. It was touch and go there last night for a while.'

'I'll tell David you rang?' suggested Li, her tone mildly speculative.

'No, there's no need,' Jacqui answered a little too definitely. 'Have a nice day!'

'You too. Are you going to Marilyn's party tomorrow night?'

'Yes. See you there. Goodbye, Li.'

Ten minutes later the phone rang.

'Jacqui.' It was David, using a very brisk tone. 'Are you all right? I'd have rung before, but I didn't want to disturb you in case you were still asleep. Li just said you'd phoned to enquire after young Malcolm Garland.'

Jacqui heaved a sigh. 'I was a bit anxious. . .'

His voice softened. 'Yes, you would be. You're a caring person, Jacqui.'

'No more than anyone else.'

He laughed and the briskness was back. 'All right, I'm embarrassing you. Now, are you quite recovered from last night's trauma?'

'Yes, of course I am.' He *was* angry with her, she thought, and unfortunately she deserved it. His next remark, however, completely floored her.

'How would you like to come ballooning tomorrow?'

'Ballooning?'

'I don't mean blowing up the party kind. I mean hot-air ballooning.' He was rushing on, trying not to give her an opportunity to say no. 'You'll love it. Quiet, peaceful, just the thing to smooth all your cares away.'

'It sounds a strange kind of therapy,' she said. 'I had no idea you could go ballooning here.'

'It's quite an attraction for locals and tourists. We have ideal conditions more often than many other places, apparently.'

'We—ell. . .' she said doubtfully.

'It's the best way to see the sunrise,' David said cheerfully.

'Sunrise?'

'Yes. That's when the air is just the right temperature and stillness. No turbulence, no thermals, no cross-draughts.'

'I haven't said I'll come.'

'It's just what you need to take your mind off unpleasant experiences.'

'But I've never done it before,' Jacqui protested. 'It sounds a bit scary.'

'Nonsense. It's as safe as being on the ground. Safer. And the view's fantastic. Come on, give it a try. You're not afraid of new adventures, are you?'

'As you discovered last night, I'm not exactly intrepid.'

'Ah, well, now's your chance to prove you can be! Ballooning isn't a health hazard like walking home after dark can be. I guarantee it'll hype you up no end.'

His mocking tone was a goad, and Jacqui laughed. 'All right, if it's doctor's orders, I suppose I can't refuse.'

'Wear something warm. It can be cold at a thousand feet.' David tried not to show his relief at her capitulation, or too great a pleasure, as he arranged the necessary dawn pick-up.

Jacqui had a few misgivings about the new experience she had allowed David to talk her into, but she didn't want to prove herself a coward by reneging on her acceptance of his invitation. Going out with him was against her resolve, but he had made it difficult for her to refuse.

It was more his concern over her experience last night that had made him invite her, she decided, than any real desire for a date with her. And ballooning scarcely counted as a date, did it? Nevertheless, she cautioned herself to be wary. David Darling had the kind of charisma that set every nerve tingling, and the memory of last night's parting kiss when he had impulsively let her hair down still sent pleasurable shivers down her spine. That too might have been merely an expression of his concern for her, a natural protectiveness stirred by her female vulnerability; nevertheless she warned herself to be careful.

It was just getting light when David arrived on Sunday morning. Jacqui was ready and waiting, and feeling more than a little apprehensive. David looked her over and nodded approvingly at the dark blue cords, white

wind-cheater and pale blue parka. She had braided her
hair and pinned the heavy plait against the back of her
head, fastening it with a clasp on top.

'I still like you better with your hair down.' David
gave her a slow smile that seemed to burst a feather
pillow in her stomach. He took her arm. 'Come on,
let's go.' He was wearing cords too and a chunky Aran-
knit sweater, both dark green. On the back seat she'd
noticed a beige parka.

After a short discussion about the asthmatic boy,
Malcolm, David said, 'By the way, I've got some good
news for you.'

'Oh, what's that?'

'The Godfreys. Mrs G has agreed to stay in town
with Joanna for a few weeks.'

Jacqui was amazed. 'Really? How did you do it?'

He turned to her with a smile. 'Charm, my dear
girl. . .just natural charm.'

'I can believe that!' She added, 'When did you see
her?'

'Yesterday afternoon. It was a heaven-sent opportunity, as it happened. She had a turn just after she
arrived and Li called me to look at her. It was clearly a
tachycardia paroxysm, and it turns out she's had a few
such "turns" lately. Her husband's illness has probably
provided the trigger. I prescribed Pronestyl, made a bit
of a fuss about her blood-pressure which is too high,
and said I really thought she ought not to drive for a
while, and that I'd like to give her an ECG and other
tests in case there's a real cardiac problem. I didn't
want to frighten her, but I think these tachycardial
spells had already been doing that, so I didn't play
them down too much. We had a chat about Wilf and in
the end she came round to agreeing to stay with Joanna

for a few weeks until her own condition was quite clear. Once we've got them settled in, I think Joanna'll be able to keep them there as long as necessary. Wilf's not going to be able to do farm work again, so a permanent move to a home unit in town might be the ultimate solution.'

'Well,' said Jacqui with emphasis, 'you seem to have wrapped that problem up. I guessed she'd listen to you.' She glanced at him, smiling. 'Thanks a lot—that's marvellous. Joanna will be delighted. She was very worried about her parents.'

David's mouth quirked a little. 'I hope you have a better impression of me now than you did at our first encounter. Have I redeemed myself from being an "arrogant cowboy"?'

Jacqui went pink. 'You heard!' She hadn't expected her muttering that evening to carry.

'I have excellent hearing,' he rejoined. 'Comes of the need in hospitals to sometimes eavesdrop on half a dozen conversations at once. Only way to keep pace with what's going on.'

'I'm sorry if I insulted you,' Jacqui apologised.

'I was a bit,' he said, assuming a hurt tone.

'It was the outfit. I never did find much to admire in the macho Aussie male swaggering about in tight jeans and broad-brimmed hat. I thought you were one of those rich, laid-back grazier types.'

He laughed. 'And what did you think when you discovered I was a doctor?'

'I thought you role-played in your leisure time!' She looked over her shoulder. 'Where's the stetson today?'

'I *was* role-playing that night! I was on my way to a cowboy party at the youth club, so I had to dress the part. The hat happens to belong to my father, likewise the check shirt. He's an old-time macho male. I don't think I'd better introduce you!'

'I was a bit mad at you that evening, but also at myself for being such an idiot backing into your car. You had every right to be angry with me, but I wasn't being very reasonable about it.'

'I was already in a foul mood,' David confessed. 'It was a trivial incident and I didn't need to bite your head off.'

She chuckled. 'We *are* baring our souls!'

And as a result perhaps now we'll get along better, David thought, but dared not say. Perhaps the barrier is down at last and she'll stop being edgy with me. He was amazed at the elation he felt at this.

'What were you in a mood about?' Jacqui asked. 'Having to dress up as a cowboy?'

He wished she hadn't asked. 'No, I didn't mind that. It was just that. . .' He paused, reluctant to reveal the truth. 'Well, let's say it was a case of an emotional argument with a—friend at the wrong moment, when I had another commitment. By the time I encountered you, I was already late, and then you wasted more time by ramming my bumper.'

Jacqui deduced that the emotional argument had probably been with a woman.

The sky was rosy and the sun almost up when they arrived at the balloon-launching site, a paddock some way out of town.

'Here we are.' David swung the car into line with others at the edge of the field.

As they got out, a huge red and yellow striped balloon rose into the still morning air, catching the first rays of the sun. Jacqui, who had never been so close to one before, gasped. She wasn't sure whether she felt nervous or excited, or both, at the prospect of her own trip.

'It's a splendid sight,' she murmured, glancing at David, who was watching the balloon, a hand shading his eyes against the brilliance of the sunrise.

He smiled at her. 'Wait till you get up there—that's the splendid sight. Quite different from how you see the world from an aircraft. You have a three-hundred-and-sixty degree panorama.

'A bird's-eye view.'

He chuckled and slid his arm across her shoulders. 'I'll introduce you to a few people before our passengers arrive.'

A car drove into the paddock and parked alongside David's. The driver got out and came over to them. He slapped David jovially on the shoulder. 'Hi, pal.'

David turned. 'Oh, hi, Kirk.' His greeting didn't carry the same enthusiasm.

Jacqui's gaze was caught and held by the newcomer's riveting light hazel eyes, and she found herself smiling at him involuntarily.

'Perfect morning for ballooning,' Kirk remarked, while not removing his attention from Jacqui.

'Yep,' said David.

'Have you been ballooning before, Miss—er——?' Kirk enquired.

'Brent,' said David crisply. 'Jacqueline Brent. Jacqui, this is Kirk Magnusson of Magnusson and Grant's Sports Goods.' He added for Kirk's benefit, 'Jacqui's a charge nurse at Lakeside. She hasn't been ballooning before.' And for her information he added, 'Kirk's our ballooning entrepreneur. He runs this show.'

Kirk Magnusson extended a hand to her. 'Delighted

to meet you, Jacqui. Don't be nervous. David is one of the best balloonists we have. He used to fly gliders, so he knows what free flight is all about.'

'I'm sure it'll be a terrific experience,' Jacqui murmured, lowering her gaze and feeling as though she had been X-rayed. She glanced at David. 'You didn't tell me you were one of the pilots.'

His mouth quirked a little. 'You might not have come!'

With a parting smile for Jacqui, Kirk strode off to where the day's customers for joy flights were gathering. It was a busy scene, with other people rushing about getting the balloons ready for take-off.

'Do you have to have a licence to fly a balloon?' Jacqui asked, still gazing aloft as she and David followed.

'Yes. It's a form of aeronautics, just like flying aircraft. The only difference is you don't come down on a runway—usually you have to be retrieved from a paddock by a four-wheel-drive.'

'What are the balloons made of?'

'A very strong nylon fabric that doesn't tear. It's held together by tough webbing.' He grinned at her intense expression. 'Really, it's quite safe. The membranes have to be replaced every few hundred hours, and they're subject to stringent checks. The safety regulations are very strict.'

Jacqui felt his confidence pass to her. 'I believe you!' She went on, 'Do you do this every weekend?'

'When I can. It's a marvellous recreation, but. . .' he patted the pocket of his parka which he had slung over one shoulder '. . .old faithful in there is inclined to call me at inconvenient moments.'

Jacqui guessed he was referring to a long-range

bleeper. 'One of the disadvantages of being a doctor,'
she commented.

'It is when you're the only permanent medico in a
hospital. You get all the emergency calls. Let's hope
everybody manages to stay well and accident-free
today, and there are no crises with patients already
admitted.'

'Are you still worried about Malcolm Garland?'
Jacqui asked, feeling a fresh twinge of anxiety.

'Let's say there are things I might tell you, but not
his mother yet,' said David. At Jacqui's look of alarm,
he went on, 'No, no, nothing critical. He's out of the
wood as far as this latest attack goes, but I'm not sure
which is the best way to maintain treatment once he
leaves us, especially while the situation at home is
likely to induce further attacks. Disodium cromo-
glycate works most of the time, using the spinhaler, as
he has been doing, but we need something more reliable
to be effective on a twenty-four-hour basis. The trouble
is there are contra-indications to cardiac conditions
with many drugs, especially some administered by
aerosol.'

'You think he has a cardiac condition?' Jacqui was
dismayed.

'Let's just say there's a little systolic murmur that
worries me. I'd like to have him checked out. I think
the best thing to do is to send him down to a specialist
in Melbourne for a short management period.'

'His mother won't be happy about that,' commented
Jacqui. 'She's a little overprotective of him, don't you
think?'

David nodded. He looked directly at Jacqui and the
corners of his mouth lifted. 'Let's not talk shop any
more. We're off duty, remember.'

Two other balloons were spread out on the ground, attached to baskets but still deflated. Jacqui felt a little thrill of nervous excitement run through her as she watched one of them gradually fill and expand, the basket straining on the rope that was attached to the front bumper of one of the four-wheel-drives to hold it down.

David introduced her to a man called Ross, who seemed to be organising the passengers. 'Yours haven't arrived yet,' he told David.

It appeared that there were actually more sightseers than passengers, and when it was time for Jacqui's flight she found herself the only passenger as those who had booked had still not turned up.

'Must have forgotten to set their alarms,' grumbled Ross, consulting his clipboard and scoring through names. 'I suppose they'll try and demand their deposit back.' He grinned at David and Jacqui. 'So, you lucky people, you've got this one all to yourselves.'

Jacqui's nervousness mounted as the moment for take-off arrived. The roaring of the gas jets, as the balloon began to inflate and rise above the wicker basket which now looked even more small and vulnerable, was alarming. Even looking up at the other colourful balloons drifting effortlessly across the vivid blue sky was not wholly reassuring. They looked immensely fragile. Jacqui was determined not to let David think she was timid, but as he helped her into the basket she managed to cross her fingers while still tightly gripping the leather-padded rim. Then, ashamed of her lack of faith in him, she uncrossed them. She'd go on to an operating table if he was operating, she thought, without a qualm about his competence, and she was sure he was as skilled at flying this thing as he was in any medical situation.

'Put this on.' David handed her a blue cap like a French Foreign Legion kepi. 'It can get a bit warm under the burner.' He was already cramming a similar cap on his own head.

There were shouts, instructions, and what seemed like temporary confusion, and then gently the balloon rose. Jacqui, intent on the huge orange and green membrane billowing above her, was unaware they were ascending until she suddenly realised that there was space between them and the ground and the collection of vehicles and people was rapidly diminishing in size.

'We're off!' she exclaimed, and it was more of a squeak of surprise than the calm observation she had meant it to be.

David turned from adjusting the burner to smile triumphantly at her. 'Around the world in eighty days, ma'am?'

'Does your bleeper work up here?' she asked.

'No. In any case, regulations say we have to have proper air-to-ground control.' He indicated the transceiver. 'Ross will let me know if I'm called. We won't be going far anyway. There's only about two hours after sunrise when it's suitable for ballooning. It's very different from gliding.' He smiled. 'That world trip will have to wait, I'm afraid.'

Jacqui was looking about her in amazement. They were more than a hundred feet off the ground now and ascending steadily. Apart from the steady noise of the burner as the flame burned the liquid petroleum gas and pushed more hot air into the colourful, bellying balloon above their heads it was stunningly quiet.

David gave a commentary on the panorama around

them. 'Look, there's Lake Maneroo and the hospital.'
He pointed in the opposite direction to where Jacqui
was looking for them. 'And over there is Hindmarsh.
Turn round and you can see the Grampians mountains
in the distance.'

'It's fantastic,' Jacqui breathed. 'All those vast paddocks and toy farmhouses, and the roads look like
black and brown ribbons. Is that a river snaking
through the trees over there?'

'A creek.'

'Those shining coffee-coloured patches, what are
they?'

'Farm dams.' He pointed again. 'Look, there are
pelicans on that one.'

'A pelican came in with the swans the other day
when I was down at the lake. He didn't care for crusts,
so I'll have to see the kitchen for spare fish.'

David slid his arm around her shoulders. 'Enjoying
it?'

She turned her face to his. 'It's fabulous. It's not
even cold.'

'We're lucky, it's a perfect morning. Too much wind
and we can't fly. If the wind is more than ten knots
we're grounded.' He smiled at the sparkle in her eyes,
and knew he wouldn't be able to resist the temptation
that he'd known being alone with her, a thousand feet
above terra firma, would invoke. He hadn't organised
to be alone in the sky with her, but Fate had kindly
delayed that family of holiday-makers to give him that
special pleasure.

He grasped her firmly and turned her into his arms.
Before she had a chance to protest he tipped both their
caps back a little to give him room to kiss her. Her
surprise showed in a sudden sharp resistance, a rigidity

in her muscles, but he didn't let that deter him. Friday night had made him impatient to repeat the exercise a little more thoroughly.

Jacqui realised that she should have half expected something like this. The trouble was she didn't have nearly enough resistance. At the first touch of his lips she froze and would have backed away except that there was nowhere to back to. She already had her back frimly against the side of the basket. She could have wrenched her face away, but she left doing it a second too long. The delicious sensation shafting through her was too powerful. Her lips lost their woodenness and relaxed against his, the rigidity of her body melted, and she let the kiss run its course. She'd had a brief taste of what kissing David would be like on Friday night. Today she knew for certain. And it was nice!

'You shouldn't have done that,' she murmured, as he broke away.

'You won't throw me overboard, I hope?' Her cheeks were flushed from the altitude and the emotion, and she looked lovelier than ever.

'Hardly? How would I get down?' She glanced at the burner. 'Shouldn't you be—er—doing things. . .?'

'In a minute.'

She was scarcely back in his arms again when the radio crackled and sprang to life. David said, 'Damn!'

'Break it up, you two.' Ross's voice, sounding amused, came through the static. 'You've had your fun, David. Duty calls. There's an emergency at Lakeside—road accident. The ambulance is on its way. A motor-cyclist has wrapped himself and his machine around a tree on an unmade road. Luckily he had a pillion passenger unhurt who went for help. Over.'

'Coming down right away,' said David. 'Thanks, Ross.'

'Sounds bad,' Jacqui commented.

David nodded. 'I thought it was too good to be true.'

'How did they know. . .?' Jacqui coloured with embarrassment.

He grinned. 'Binoculars. Ross bird-watches and he keeps an eye on the balloons too.'

'Is kissing against the rules?'

He rubbed his nose against hers and drifted his lips casually across her mouth. 'Not that I know of.'

'Do you do it often?' Suddenly she felt hollow inside. Did David take every new girlfriend ballooning? Was the absence of other passengers merely an excuse, and he organised lone flights on purpose? Thinking about it made the experience lose some of its magic.

He was busy with the burner now, reducing the air pressure in the balloon. He glanced over his shoulder. 'I've never kissed a girl in a balloon before,' he said, meeting her eyes steadily for a moment, and giving the impression he was reading her mind. 'Usually I have three or four passengers. This is a commercial enterprise. There really were people who had booked but who didn't turn up.'

Jacqui felt rebuked, but she still wasn't sure whether to believe him. She kept silent while David controlled their descent. She saw two four-wheel-drive vehicles racing across the paddock where they would touch down. For a moment it seemed they would crash into the middle of a dam, but David controlled the balloon expertly and they skimmed over the top of it. The basket touched earth with scarcely a bump and listed to one side.

David helped Jacqui out, and, while two ground

crew retrieved the balloon, he took the wheel of the other vehicle and they bumped back over the paddocks to the launch site which fortunately was not far away.

'Sorry about this, Jacqui,' David said before getting into his own car. He pressed her arm and seemed reluctant to let go. 'I was hoping to buy you a slap-up breakfast.'

Kirk Magnusson came up to them. He had overheard David's remark and said, 'There's no need for Jacqui to rush off. She can have breakfast with us and I'll run her home later.'

Jacqui suspected that 'us' really meant with him alone. She hesitated, not sure what David would want her to say. He was looking at her, but the dark blue eyes had no easily readable message for her. So she made her own decision. 'I think I'll go too, thank you all the same, Kirk,' she said.

David was already behind the wheel, so she slid quickly in beside him. Kirk Magnusson clasped her shoulder briefly before slamming the car door. 'Some other time, maybe,' he murmured.

'You could have stayed,' said David as the car sped out of the paddock and headed back to town. 'There's probably time for another trip.' He sounded cool all at once.

'I didn't want another trip. I've already had a fabulous time.'

There was silence for a moment or two, then he said rather brusquely, 'Magnusson fancies you.'

'Does he? He's only just met me.'

'He's the local Don Juan, you know.'

His attitude nettled her. 'No, I didn't. I thought you had that distinction.'

He gave her a sharp look. 'Who's been bending your ear?'

'No one. It's easy to see you're popular with women.'

'You seem to imply your own exclusion.'

He sounded gritty, and Jacqui was puzzled. Maybe it was just because he was wondering what kind of emergency the accident victim would prove to be, how badly smashed up he might be. It could be a case of calling the air ambulance to take him down to Melbourne.

Back in town, she insisted that David drop her off at the top of her street. She walked slowly down the tree-lined avenue and around the house to her flat. For her the excursion had ended in a kind of anticlimax, but it had certainly been an experience to remember.

She met Elsa carrying a basketload of washing to the clothes hoist in the rear garden.

'Hi there,' Elsa greeted her. 'You look pretty pleased with yourself.'

'Do I?' Jacqui was bemused.

'You must have gone out early.'

'At dawn. I've been ballooning.' Jacqui had a feeling people would get to know quite quickly, so she might as well be honest about it.

'Really? You're game. Not with our resident Prince Charming?'

'If you mean David, well, yes. . .'

Elsa hooted. 'I wonder what Rina will think of that! She'll find out, of course. Nothing's private in Maneroo.'

'Who's Rina?' Jacqui's mouth felt dry.

'His on-off beloved. Didn't you know? The gossips have been slipping up. Let's have a coffee and I'll fill you in.'

Jacqui was angry with herself for being curious, but she couldn't help it. She invited Elsa in and made coffee. Elsa was only too happy to impart what she knew.

Rina Parkinson was the daughter of a local retired dentist. Her parents, it appeared, had gone overseas on the same trip as the Darlings.

'Rina's the temperamental type,' Elsa said. 'She's also a cracker to look at, all dark, sultry and sexy. It's a pretty stormy relationship, apparently.' She shook her finger at Jacqui. 'Don't you go falling for him, Jacqui. He'll break your heart if you do.' She sighed. 'He's the kind of man it's all too easy to fall for, I'm afraid.'

Jacqui had to agree that Elsa was right. David was the kind of man it would be all too easy to fall for. Like Carey. She shuddered at the memory of her mistake. David wasn't wholly like Carey, of that she felt certain, but she must still be careful. No more dates with David Darling, she told herself emphatically. Which, she realised at once, was tantamount to admitting that already he had made a greater impression on her than was comfortable.

CHAPTER FIVE

ON MONDAY morning Jacqui forced herself to take the short cut to the hospital. It was no good becoming paranoid about the prowler. She would, however, never be foolish or careless enough to walk home that way in the dark again. It just wasn't worth the risk.

Nevertheless, she could not help shuddering at the thought of what might have happened had she reached the turn-off to the back lane which was only accessible on foot, before she'd seen the prowler—*if* she had seen anyone. If he hadn't overtaken her by the time he reached the entrance gates, would David have guessed she must have taken the short cut? In her bones she felt he would have checked. David Darling was that sort of man. He followed up, paid attention to detail. It showed in his attitude to medicine, and she was sure it would be paramount in his personal life. She was coming to realise that David Darling was a man who cared very much about people.

When she walked into the nurses' room to change into her uniform, her mind was also more than a little preoccupied with last night's party. Marilyn Field was on Maternity and Jacqui had only spoken to her a couple of times, but it seemed that when anyone threw a party it was open invitation to the whole nursing staff to go.

Jacqui had gone with the girls from the house and she'd had a good time in a fashion. Everyone had been very friendly. Most of the nurses had brought boyfriends or husbands, and there had been a sprinkling of unattached males to make up numbers.

Although she'd enjoyed dancing in the Fields' enormous living-room with several different partners, her mind had kept wandering back to the morning's ballooning with David, and her skin had still tingled at the memory of his kiss. Talk about head in the clouds! She was mad to have let him kiss her like that. . .

Halfway through the evening, standing near the doorway to the patio for a little fresh air, she'd heard Marilyn, who was just outside, saying to someone, 'Yes, of course I asked David to come. But I don't suppose he will. He was called in to an emergency this morning. He was out ballooning. Guess who with? Jacqui Brent.'

There was surprised laughter. 'I knew he saved her from a fate worse than death on Friday night. The hospital has been buzzing with that piece of news all weekend.' There was a slight pause. 'Does she know about Rina?' It was a female voice Jacqui could not put a name to.

'I don't know,' said Marilyn. 'But when Rina gets wind of the ballooning episode, she probably soon will! Rina's not the sort to take kindly to having what she considers her preserves poached upon.'

The other girl said, 'Some time ago Rina told my sister she was finished with David for good, but that's happened before and she doesn't mean it. She's really crazy about him.' She added thoughtfully, 'I wonder if he's trying to make her jealous.'

'Well, I hope he isn't using Jacqui. She seems very nice and everyone seems to get on well with her.'

'So I've heard. She's efficient but not bossy. I hope

she stays on after Marion gets back, and takes Greta's place. Greta will be about ready to leave to have her baby then.' There followed a couple of comments about Greta, then Marilyn said, 'Let's go back inside.'

Jacqui had moved away hastily, not sure whether it was more embarrassing to hear bad things about one-self or good. It was the first time she had ever eaves-dropped on a conversation about herself, and it gave her a guilty feeling.

She'd been glad when two of the other girls from the house had decided to leave the party. Like her, Elsa and Donna were on early next day. Jennie's boyfriend would be taking her home.

'Marilyn will organise a lift for you, Jacqui,' Donna, who had driven them to the party, had said. 'You don't have to leave now too.'

But Jacqui had been glad to go. After hearing Marilyn say she had invited David, she'd found herself watching doorways with the sort of faint hope that made her feel ashamed of herself. David wasn't going to turn up, and in any case she didn't want to be there if he did.

Now, hurrying along to her office to take over from Li, she wasn't sure she was looking forward to seeing David today. She must try not to feel awkward with him. What if he had been using her? She'd had a marvellous experience going up in a balloon which she wouldn't have missed for worlds. And after all, kissing a person was no big deal, not even in a hot-air balloon.

Nevertheless, going out with him on Sunday had given a new dimension to their relationship, tilting it from the professional over into the personal. It might be difficult now to re-establish that safe cool distance that had existed between them previously. David might be a devious flirt who used women for his own ends, but Jacqui did not want even to appear to be poaching on someone else's territory, and from what she'd heard it certainly looked as though David was definitely still Rina's. It was more than likely he'd meant news of their date, and that kiss conveniently staged for Ross to observe through binoculars, to get back to her. If there had been a rift, no doubt he was hoping for a reconciliation.

Li greeted Jacqui in her usual quiet but friendly manner. She was small and dark with grave almond eyes and a serene expression that was occasionally transformed by a spontaneous smile. She was a refugee from Vietnam and had not had a great deal to smile about in her life. In her precise, low-toned voice, she updated Jacqui on the patients, including two new admissions.

'Mrs Manton has an ulcerated leg and may have to be transferred to Surgical, but they're full up at the moment, and Mr Paget has food poisoning.' She gave one of her rare smiles. 'He blames his wife. He says she put tinned cat food on his toast instead of Vegemite because he stayed out late at the RSL Club on Saturday night.' She giggled. 'David says, since no one else who ate at the club seems to be ill, it's probably true!'

Jacqui chuckled. 'We certainly get some characters.'

'It's a nice hospital,' said Li with simple sincerity. 'I shall be sorry to leave.'

'You're leaving?' Jacqui was taken aback.

'I just meant when Lakeside closes,' Li explained. 'I don't know whether I will go to Hindmarsh if they offer me a job there. My family are here now and my mother needs me to help with my brothers and sisters. It will be a long drive to commute to Hindmarsh. I don't know yet what I will do. Maybe we will all have to move to the bigger town.' She shrugged resignedly.

'It might not happen,' said Jacqui. 'From what I've heard, a lot of people are in favour of keeping Lakeside open.'

Li shrugged. 'We will have to wait and see.'

As usual the changeover of shifts was smooth, with little time wasted. Jacqui's briefings were always just that, brief, but to the point, and soon the ward was humming again with activity as medications were dispensed, bed calls answered, and the hundred and one necessary tasks were carried out.

Jacqui liked to have everything ticking over smoothly by the time David came on his rounds. She had sensed early on that seeing people dashing about rather obviously catching up with tasks suggested poor organisation to him, so she endeavoured to create an atmosphere of calm competence, at least whenever he was around. Chaos did have a habit of disrupting the most orderly of regimes, and her ward was no exception at times.

The first thing Jacqui did herself was to check on all her patients, and especially Malcolm, the asthmatic boy. She was delighted to find him sitting up in bed, out of the oxygen tent now, and doing a large jigsaw with his mother.

'Hello, Malcolm, how are you today?' she enquired. 'I'm Jacqui.'

'Say hello to Sister,' his mother prompted. 'She's the one who took care of you on Friday.'

'Not only me! I was here on Friday, but I've been off duty over the weekend,' Jacqui explained.

'Oh, hi,' said the boy, and gave her a slow smile. His large eyes still had the staring glassy look of the asthmatic and there were dark rings beneath them, but his colour was more normal and there was only a slight wheeze in his breathing. He would still be pretty exhausted, Jacqui knew. He was a good-looking child with a mop of dark hair and, like many asthmatic children, he was probably above average intelligence, and doubtless highly sensitive too. She wondered if David had spoken to his mother yet about sending Malcolm to a specialist in Melbourne.

Mrs Garland said, 'He gave us all a bit of a fright, didn't he, Sister? But Dr Darling fixed him up. He's going to be fine now. We've got some new medicine that'll stop those nasty attacks before they start.'

'I've got to use a—a nebuliser,' Malcolm informed Jacqui. 'And Dr Darling is experimenting on me with different drugs because I'm a pretty bad case.' He grinned proudly.

Jacqui hid a smile. She didn't think David was experimenting on the ten-year-old exactly, but suspected that making Malcolm feel important might be his way of leading up to the visit to the specialist in Melbourne. She glanced at her watch. 'It's time you showed me how you use the nebuliser,' she said.

She lingered for a few minutes, allowing herself to indulge the satisfaction that always came with seeing patients get better, especially when they'd been in a critical condition. And especially when the patient was a child.

At ten-thirty, prompt as always, David arrived. Jacqui found him suddenly at her side as she pored over some case notes, her back to the door, and jumped. 'Oh. . .you startled me!'

'Sorry.' The dark blue eyes engaged hers for a

moment, and he smiled. 'Even more sorry I had to abandon you yesterday.'

'You don't have to apologise for emergencies. Was it bad?'

'Dead on arrival,' he said, lips tightening. 'Another statistic.'

'Sad.'

'Yes. He was only twenty-two.' He took a deep breath. 'Right, shall we start?'

Doing the round with him wasn't as bad as Jacqui had imagined. David was as brisk and professional as ever. He made no mention of the intimacy in the balloon, or even spoke about their date again at all. Jacqui deliberately kept the conversation to clinical matters regarding the patients, and was purposely impersonal with him. She didn't want him to think that because he'd invited her out once they were now on a different footing, or that he had any obligation to invite her out again, or even to get the idea that she wanted him to. Nevertheless, she felt that there was a new rapport between them now, that because of Friday and Sunday they knew each other a little better, were more at ease together.

'Coffee?' she enquired as they returned to her office where he usually enlarged on his requirements for individual patients, signed discharges, and answered any questions she might have that it had not been tactful to ask in front of patients.

'Thanks,' he said as usual, and made himself comfortable in her armchair.

She had installed an electric coffee-maker in her office and had left a brew to filter while they were occupied on the ward. She poured him a cup and set it on the desk near him. They talked medical matters for some minutes and Jacqui made the necessary notes on her pad. At one point she couldn't resist saying,

'You don't have to dot all the "i"s and cross all the "t"s, you know. We nurses are trained to do quite a lot on our own initiative.'

It was only a gentle rebuke, delivered with a smile, but he looked put out. 'Are you suggesting I'm telling you how to do your job?'

'No! But you're so meticulous, David. You seem to think you're responsible for every little detail.'

He raked his hair back and laughed wryly. 'You're right. At least two of my professors told me I needed to learn how to delegate. It's a bad fault.'

It was a measure of the progress in their relationship, Jacqui thought, that she dared to talk to him in this way. 'There are worse ones,' she said. 'But if you try to close every loophole yourself, you end up overworking.' He looked tired and she guessed he hadn't had much sleep all weekend, but whether that was the hospital's fault or Rina's she tried not to speculate. She reminded herself that it had been purely gossip she had overheard about him and Rina.

He said half seriously, 'I hope you're not going to prove too militant.'

'It's occasionally necessary to remind doctors that nurses have brains and have undergone years of training too.'

'Ouch! You never told me you were a feminist.'

'I'm not. At least, not a rabid one.'

His eyes showed a lively humour. 'But you're not just a pretty face!'

Jacqui assumed a stern expression. 'That was a *very* sexist remark, Dr Darling!' She added, 'You doubted my competence at first.'

He looked at her with real regret. 'Yes, and I'm sorry. You've more than proved how wrong I was. I don't think we've ever had such a conscientious charge nurse at Lakeside.'

Jacqui grimaced. 'Oh, *please*! I wasn't fishing for compliments.' She nevertheless felt warmed by his words, if not entirely deserving.

'No, but I owe you an apology.'

'You've already explained why you were prickly that night at the garage.' Then she laughed. 'How did we get on to this?'

'You took umbrage at my saying the obvious about something I've now completely forgotten.'

'I didn't take umbrage, and, if your short-term memory is failing that badly, you really are overworking.'

His eyes darkened sensuously. 'My short-term memory is pretty good,' he drawled. 'I remember kissing a not altogether unwilling redhead in a balloon only twenty-four hours ago. It was a very pleasant experience. I was wondering when it might be repeated.'

'The ballooning?' Jacqui's face was pink.

'You know I meant the kiss.' He rose swiftly, pulled her from her chair into his arms and translated the desire into instant action.

'David, really!' She struggled ineffectually. 'Someone might come!'

'All the more reason not to waste time,' he said huskily.

Jacqui felt her limbs soften and her body moulded itself to his in spite of herself. She yearned for the kiss as much as he did. For blissful seconds warm lips blended in the gentlest but most sensual massage. When a deeper passion sparked, she pulled away.

'I don't think you should do that,' she said. 'And I'm not in the habit of poaching on other people's preserves.'

He looked at her for a long moment, lips tightly together. 'Oh-oh, somebody's been telling you about Rina Parkinson.'

'It's hardly a secret, is it?'

He leaned against the wall, drumming his fingers on it. 'The trouble with small towns is, if the doctor sneezes, everyone knows in half an hour. Bush telegraph is a fact of life.' He looked at her solemnly. 'I guess I have to tell you about Rina myself.'

'Of course you don't. Your love-life is nothing to do with me, but if kissing me in public helps it, then I'll overlook that liberty.' But not the present one, she implied.

His hands moved restlessly up and down her arms. 'It's rather complicated. There isn't time to explain now. Have dinner with me one night this week?'

Jacqui shook her head. 'Thanks, but no, thanks.'

He seemed taken aback at her refusal. 'Jacqui, why not?'

'I'd rather not, that's all.'

He looked grim. 'All right, I'll explain now.'

'It won't make any difference.'

There was a tap on the door and an anxious-faced Angela looked in. 'Oh—sorry.'

'Is something the matter?' Jacqui asked at once.

'It's Mrs DiMaggio. She was supposed to be OK to go to the bathroom by herself, and young Pauline's just found her fallen over in one of the cubicles. . .'

David and Jacqui rushed out with her. In the

women's toilet they found the nursing aide, Pauline, very distraught because she and Angela hadn't been able to shift the elderly woman, who was groaning, and clearly stressed. It was a simple matter, however, for David to extricate the patient from the space between the pedestal and the wall.

'Thank goodness we refitted all our existing toilets with outward opening doors and no locks, when the annexe was built,' he said, 'or we might have had a job getting to her.'

Mrs DiMaggio was dazed but unhurt and she was able to stand with assistance. It seemed she had not collapsed but had slipped and because of her over-weight had not been able to pull herself up. The two nurses had been unable to move her from her awkward position, and had been fearful she might have injured herself.

'I was wondering how she could possibly go into a coma,' said Jacqui, after they had put the old lady back to bed. 'She had a near normal urine test this morning.'

'She'll have a few bruises.' David had again accompanied Jacqui to her office. 'Diabetics bruise easily, as you know, so keep an eye on them in case pressure sores develop.'

Jacqui said, 'It was lucky you were still here. Thanks for your help.'

He grinned. 'Male muscles do have their uses!'

She tingled, recalling how only minutes ago he had held her tightly. 'Well, don't you think you ought to see if they're needed elsewhere? I've got a lot of work to do.' The truth was, he was making her feel edgy.

He touched her shoulder lightly. 'Will you have dinner with me? Say Thursday.' When she began to shake her head, he went on persuasively, 'There's something else I want to talk to you about. About the hospital. A project I need your help with.'

He certainly had a way of getting around people. She said, 'David Darling, you are incorrigible!'

It probably meant, she thought later, that he'd never get around to explaining about Rina, if there really was anything to explain. And even if he told her so, Jacqui wasn't sure she could believe that he was no longer entangled, or that he didn't want to be, with the girl. Look at the way Carey had behaved.

Jacqui was all ready to go out on Thursday evening when David phoned. He had an urgent case to attend to and couldn't make it. She put the phone down with a resigned sigh. Dating a doctor was rarely straightforward. She was kicking her shoes off and about to change back into comfortable clothes before switching on the television when Elsa appeared.

'Hi, Jacqui. You wouldn't like to go to the flicks, would you? Donna and I were going and then she had to do a double shift.' She noticed that Jacqui was dressed to go out. 'Oh, you're going out.' She sounded disappointed.

'No, I'm not. Not now.'

Elsa gave her a curious look. 'Date cancelled?' When Jacqui nodded, she queried, 'David?'

'Yes, as a matter of fact.' There was no point in prevaricating.

'Never date a doctor,' intoned Elsa. 'They always let you down.'

'Not their fault.'

'Not always. Some use it as an excuse.' Elsa added hastily, 'Not David, I'm sure. Well, would you like to go? It's a bit grim stopping in alone and there's a good show on, that new Glenda Jackson picture.'

Jacqui didn't mind stopping in alone, but as she was already dressed she decided she might as well go to the film. She didn't see a lot of the girls in the other part of the house and hoped they didn't think she was stand-offish, or unapproachable because she was senior to them. It was just that they seemed to lead hectic social lives and were rarely at home when she was.

'OK,' she said. 'It sounds like good idea. Shall we eat out first? I haven't got much food in.'

Elsa was delighted. 'Oh, good, I'm so glad. I was feeling a bit depressed and it looked like a long dreary evening ahead. Let's go to Mario's. You like Italian food, don't you?'

'Love it!'

Mario's was small and intimate. There were high-backed booths along both sides and tables and chairs down the middle. It was early and not crowded yet, so Jacqui and Elsa were able to get a booth to themselves.

'How's Physio these days?' Jacqui asked as they began on their huge plates of lasagne.

Elsa pulled a face. 'I don't know what got into me, doing physiotherapy. Just because I was keen on sport at school!'

'It must be pretty satisfying, though.'

Elsa groaned. 'You're joking! If you'd ever tried to get great strapping farmer footballers to do exercises, you'd know. Oh, they like all the thumping and mas-saging, but help themselves. . .' She rolled her eyes at the ceiling, then grinned. 'It's not so bad really. I had three very querulous cartilage jobs to rehabilitate this week, and an Achilles tendon, and a back strain, which is why I'm moaning.' She paused, giving her dark head a nonchalent toss. 'And believe me, passes don't only happen with a ball during the game!'

Jacqui laughed. 'I'm sure you know how to keep them in order.'

'Thank goodness the football season is over, cricket isn't quite so bad.'

'For injuries or flirtation?'

'Both,' said Elsa firmly.

'How are you getting on with young Malcolm?' Jacqui asked.

'Fine. He's great—intelligent kid. He's the sort who won't let asthma make an invalid of him. His hero is Allan Border—you know, he captained the Australian side in the test series in England?'

'Vaguely. I'm not much of a follower of cricket.'

'Well, Malcolm aims to play cricket for Australia one day, so he'll do anything to achieve it. Amazingly, quite a few top sportsmen are asthmatic, so there's no reason why he shouldn't go for it.'

'David wants to send him down to Melbourne for a couple of weeks, under a specialist,' said Jacqui.

'Good idea,' said Elsa.

Jacqui nodded and they discussed Malcolm's illness and his home life for a few minutes, drifting on to other topics until Elsa glanced at her watch and said, 'Finish your coffee, then we'd better go, or we'll miss the trailers and the cartoon!'

As Jacqui lifted her cup to drain it, she glanced across to the other side of the restaurant. The tables and the booths were almost all full now. A small group of people were about to sit down, and when they did she had an oblique view of the booth right at the back on the other side. She caught her breath. Surely. . .surely that was David?

'What's up, seen a ghost?' Elsa had spotted the change in her expression that Jacqui hadn't been able to hide. She looked around and then said in a low, sympathetic voice, 'That's Rina Parkinson with him.'

'I thought it must be.' Jacqui hoped her voice didn't reveal the shattering effect seeing David and the other woman together was having on her. He had said he had an urgent case, and she had assumed he meant at the hospital. He had meant her to assume that, which was the same as lying to her. Rina had laid claim to him, and she had had first priority. It was Carey all over again. Well, it was only to be expected. What was unexpected was her reaction to catching him out, the sick, hollow feeling inside her that she recognised as jealousy.

Elsa said gently, 'Don't take him too seriously, Jacqui.'

Jacqui forced a smile. 'I don't! I had a feeling,' she lied, 'that his excuse wasn't quite genuine.'

'Men are so-and-sos,' said Elsa. 'Come on, let's go. Do you want him to see you?'

'Heavens, no!'

'Why not? It'd give him a jolt if you waltzed over and said hello, introduce me to your charming emergency!'

That was the last thing Jacqui wanted to do. She had no desire to meet the slender, rather fragile-looking girl who was talking earnestly to David. She had a pale, elfin face framed by straight dark hair, and enormous eyes. She was beautiful in a rather gaunt kind of way. Her head was nearly touching David's across the table. It looked a very intimate tête-à-tête.

Later, Jacqui was sure that the film had been excellent, but she could remember very little of it. Between her and the screen kept intruding images of two people, one of whom had broken a date with her to dine with another woman. Just the way Carey must have done a score of times.

She invited Elsa in for coffee afterwards and they chatted till midnight. When Jacqui went to bed, for the first time in quite a while, she wept for being such a gullible fool—again.

David was not in the next day. The story was that he'd had some sudden urgent business to attend to in Melbourne and would be away for a couple of days. Jacqui could not get it out of her head that the urgent business must be to do with Rina Parkinson, and that ring-buying might be part of it.

He breezed into her office two mornings later, and the first thing he did was to apologise for the broken date. Two-timers were always good at that, she reflected, recalling Carey once more. They turned on the charm and expected all to be forgiven.

Jacqui wondered if it would be possible to tell by looking at a person if he had got engaged. David didn't look any different. But men didn't ever look starry-eyed, did they? she thought. They were too cold and calculating, and devious!

'There's no need to apologise,' she said stiffly. 'Duty is duty. I've had to do the same myself sometimes.' She made her mouth stretch into a brief dismissive smile.

He frowned. 'You're cross with me, though.'

'Of course I'm not.'

'I had to go to Melbourne on some—er—personal business,' he said. 'I didn't have time to call you first.'

She affected surprise. 'There's no reason why you should have.'

'You're very frosty this morning,' he complained, raising an eyebrow.

'You're imagining things. Shall we start with the men or the women today?' She picked up her clipboard and angled a querying look at him.

'The women,' he said indifferently.

As she moved towards the door, he seemed about to say something more, and Jacqui paused expectantly, but only saw him clamp his lips together in a tight line. He followed her out.

Women, he thought, were so unpredictable. Her offhandedness irked him more than it should have done. He'd been going to suggest an alternative date, but he'd sensed she would make an excuse. In the past two days he'd lost all the progress he'd made with her and she'd hardened even more against him. He followed her straight-backed progress along the corridor, shoulders square in her immaculate lilac linen jacket, shapely hips swinging, her bright hair tamed into submission by hairpins and a clasp, and his throat was dry as he remembered running his fingers through that loosened glossy mane.

'Sharon Walker was admitted yesterday,' Jacqui informed him as they went into the first room. 'She's a patient of Dr Prentiss. Acute pyelitis. She's allergic to penicillin, so she's on Bactrim now. Her fever's down and her pulse-rate's normal. Dr Prentiss is coming in today and he wants to see you.'

She did not look at David while she was speaking. In fact she avoided looking at him during the whole time he was on her ward. She cultivated and maintained as distant a manner as possible, and she was hardly surprised when, instead of accompanying her back to her office for their usual cup of coffee, he made an excuse.

'We've got three mums in labour this morning and I might have to do a Caesar on one. If you've any queries, call me later.' With his usual swish of coat-tails and without even a ghost of a smile, he was gone.

Jacqui bit her lip and stared out through her window down to the lake. She couldn't see any swans today, or pelicans, but there were plenty of black ducks pottering around the reedy edges. The water was calm and reflected the brilliant blue sky like a mirror.

'Pull yourself together,' she admonished herself. 'You're not in so deep that you can't save yourself from drowning!'

CHAPTER SIX

IT WAS back to square one, Jacqui thought a few days later, and wondered why she didn't feel a little more thankful for that. The greater professional rapport between her and Dr Darling remained, which was gratifying, but on the personal level they were back to being no more than friendly colleagues.

David did not invite her out again. At all times he was polite but detached. Sometimes he seemed to be looking right through her when she was speaking to him, as though half his mind was somewhere else. With Rina, Jacqui surmised, trying to quell her curiosity about that relationship.

Most days Jacqui still took her sandwiches down to the lake at lunchtime, but David never joined her. Until, one day a few weeks later, when she was eating her lunch and reading a letter she'd received from Malcolm Garland, and he was for once absent from her mind. When a shadow fell across the bench and she glanced around to see David standing there, plastic-wrapped sandwiches and paper cup of coffee in his hands, her heart gave a leap of pleasure.

'Mind if I join you?'

His smile was warm, but his eyes a little anxious. It was like a replay of a film.

'Of course not. It's a public bench!' She tried for a light tone, but a quaver in her voice spoilt it. His unexpected appearance had caused more internal confusion than she would have thought possible. After all, she saw him practically every day, had accompanied him on a ward round that very morning. Usually she saw him in a white coat. Now, in the light grey trousers and darker grey open-neck shirt he'd been wearing under it, he looked less like the professional medico she was accustomed to dealing with, and altogether too much like the man who had once kissed her in a balloon.

David sat down. He was probably mad invading her lunch hour like this, but looking at her solitary figure through his office window as he so often did, and feeling jealous when anyone else, even one of the other nurses, joined her, had finally goaded him. Before he knew what he was doing, he was again buying sandwiches from the canteen and helping himself to coffee from the machine, ready to risk her cold shoulder.

There was an awkward pause. Eventually Jacqui said, 'I had a thank-you letter from Malcolm Garland today. You remember, the boy with asthma who resented his mother's man-friend?'

'Yes, of course I remember. Mrs Garland eventually agreed to let him go down to Melbourne to the Royal Children's. The last I heard, from his GP, was that he was pretty well stabilised on a combination of Berotec and Atrovent. There was also some psychiatric counselling of the mother and the boy, I believe.'

'Which seems to have had a good effect,' Jacqui observed, handing him the letter. 'Read what he says about Steve.'

'The mother's boyfriend?' David read the letter while Jacqui contemplated the lake and tossed her remaining crumbs to the semicircle of ducks.

'Amazing,' he commented, handing it back. 'He's actually pleased they're getting married. And good on

Steve, going to watch him play cricket and teaching him to windsurf. Obviously they're both keen on sport, so it looks as if a happy compromise has been reached.'

'Which may mean fewer asthma attacks.'

'Let's hope so.'

Jacqui folded the letter and put it in her pocket. Conversation seemed to have been exhausted. She couldn't even think of anything concerning a patient that she wanted to talk to him about. Finally, when the silence began to make her edgy, she chose a time-honoured stopgap. 'Weather's warmer,' she commented, lifting her gaze to the clear blue sky.

It was his turn to feed the ducks and swans, which he did with concentration, not glancing at her when he answered, 'Yes. How do you like Australian summers?'

Just like that first time he joined me here, we're so stilted, Jacqui thought. 'Last summer wasn't very hot, at least not in Melbourne. It rained a lot. We had so many grey days, sometimes I felt I might as well be at home.'

'If you want hot weather, you should go to Sydney, Adelaide or Perth,' David told her. 'Melbourne's climate is almost English. You'll find it's hotter up in this part of Victoria, though.'

'I think I'll enjoy that.'

'Missing the big city yet?' Brushing crumbs off his hands, he glanced at her with the first evidence of a smile.

'No. I've amazed myself as well as my friends back in Melbourne and my folks in England. They all said I was a dyed-in-the-wool city slicker, but it seems there was a frustrated little country girl inside just waiting to break out!' She laughed at herself, and he chuckled.

'You could stay on here for as long as you want, you know.'

'Yes. Matron mentioned that Greta will be leaving to have a baby soon after Marion gets back. I like it at Lakeside, but I'm not sure I'd want to move to Hindmarsh when they close the hospital here.'

'Lakeside won't be closing,' David said emphatically, as he had once before.

'Won't it? But only the other day I heard. . .'

He screwed up the plastic from around his sand-wiches and aimed the ball at the waste bin, scoring a goal. 'A few weeks ago, you might recall, I mentioned asking for your help.'

Jacqui remembered. He had been going to talk about it, whatever it was, on that date which had been cancelled. 'My help? Is it to do with the hospital? How can I help?'

He turned towards her, hitching one leg on to the bench and grasping his ankle. 'I think you'd make a good organiser.'

'Thanks! What do you want me to organise?'

'I've been busy doing a bit of grass roots polling,' he told her. 'I'm convinced that the people of Maneroo, given a choice, will say no to closing Lakeside. It's not a big hospital, but it does provide local people with work, not just for nurses, but in the administration, supplies and services areas. The town is growing with a steady annual increase in tourism, so it's going to need more, not less health care.'

'But Hindmarsh is being built to cope with all that, isn't it?'

'When they finish it!' he said rather scathingly. 'At the moment there's a shortage of funds and they're cutting corners all over the place. Industrial relations aren't good on site either. Goodness knows when it'll be open. And when it is, there'll be demands on it from other nearby places besides Maneroo, places that haven't got the facilities we have.'

'I thought the council here was committed to closing Lakeside and selling the land for a tourist complex,' Jacqui remarked.

He gave her a telling look. 'It hasn't actually been passed yet. There's no contract with anyone. One or two people in the town stand to benefit directly, so a fair bit of lobbying has been going on and it's come up at council meetings, but the decision still needs to be made officially. Before that happens we need to get the waverers on our side.'

'I don't see how I can help to do that.'

'You can help me to organise our Open Day. I want it to be a real propaganda day this year. We'll get everyone fired up about losing the hospital, show them graphically why they need to keep it, and then we'll take a stack of petitions to the council and the Health Department and show them that public opinion is against the closure. It's my guess that we can get most of Maneroo and surrounding districts to sign a petition against the scheme. The council and the Government will have to take notice.'

'I imagine a lot of business people are in favour of the tourist complex,' said Jacqui doubtfully. 'It will bring more business to the town.'

'There can still be a tourist complex,' said David. 'There's land on the other side of the lake that the owner is now willing to sell.' He pointed in the general direction he was referring to. 'Plenty of room for a golf course.'

'It's a fair way from the town centre.'

'Which is a good place for it to be,' David said
forcefully. 'Then they won't be encroaching on the
public's right to use the lake near to town. That's a
right we should preserve.'

'Have the developers been offered that alternative?'

'They're not interested in alternatives while there's a
chance they can get this prime site at a favourable
price.'

'So you intend to use people-power to change the
bureaucratic mind and persuade the Government to
find the funds for Lakeside as well as Hindmarsh?
That's a tall order.'

'I don't think so. First we convince people that they
need Lakeside as well as Hindmarsh hospital, then they
convince the Government. Will you help, Jacqui?'

'What do you want me to do?'

'Open Day is next month,' he said. 'It's going to be
the biggest and best we've ever had, and we're going
to leave no emotional stone unturned in the fight to
retain Lakeside, I promise you.'

'I admire your confidence!' Jacqui looked at him,
puzzled. 'But why are you so passionate about it,
David? How can it matter to you? You could move up
into a consultant's job if you went to Hindmarsh.'

He shrugged. 'I don't like to see the real needs of
people relegated so that vested interests can make a
fast buck. I don't like to see ordinary people manipu-
lated, exploited or brushed aside. And they will be in
this town unless someone organises them to stick up
for their right to a hospital service right here in
Maneroo when they're sick. We have to show them
that that's more important than the healthy tourist's
right to luxury accommodation and priority use of the

lake.' He stopped and a smile tugged his mouth awry.
'I suppose I sound like rabble-rouser!'

'You sound very practical, and fierce enough to
convince anybody.' And, Jacqui thought, he has the
charisma to achieve his ends. 'You've convinced me,'
she laughed.

'Just about everyone in this town has needed the
hospital at some time or another,' said David. 'So we
should be able to get a high percentage of them on our
side. The rest we'll persuade.'

'Won't your stand make it awkward for you? I mean,
if there are some influential people who don't like what
you're doing, they might try to have you removed.'

He acknowledged that danger. 'I think they'd have
difficulty, though, in terminating my contract.' He
grinned. 'I'll worry about that if it happens.'

Jacqui suddenly realised that time was slipping away.
She rose quickly. 'I'd better get back.'

They walked up to the hospital together, with David
still expounding his plans enthusiastically. It was as
though he had been bottling it all up and today, with
her, the floodgates had opened. She felt mildly
flattered.

'Keep it all under your hat for the moment,' he
cautioned before they parted to go their separate ways.
'We don't want the opposition to know what we're
about until we spring it on them. I'll be getting a few
people together quite soon to map out the specifics of
the campaign. Will you come to the meeting?' He
looked at her anxiously. Her face was slightly flushed
from the hour in the fresh air, her satiny skin tantalising
his fingers which itched to frame it gently, while his
mouth. . . He desperately wanted to be with her somewhere very private, but he didn't dare to suggest a

date. Enlisting her aid was daring enough. She'd agreed to help, but he felt it was probably only because she didn't know how to refuse.

'Yes, of course I will. I only hope I'll be as useful as you seem to think.' If he touches me now, she thought, if he just leans over the few inches needed and kisses me, I'll forgive him everything, and I won't even ask questions about Rina.

'Jacqui. . .' He spoke her name in a breathless rush, and the moment she had been imagining seemed to have arrived. He leaned towards her and his arms half rose to reach out to her. But they were in a public space and the sound of footsteps on the polished linoleum floor of an adjacent corridor broke the spell.

'I'll let you know where and when,' he said, and, in his usual decisive way, walked off.

The footsteps materialised into Angela. 'Oh, hi,' she said cheerily, and, staring after the figure disappearing along the other corridor, 'Was that David?'

'Mmm.' Jacqui was still a little bemused, still half caught in the magic aura that had enmeshed her moments ago.

Angela looked at Jacqui's pink cheeks. 'Well, either the fresh air or the doctor gives you a healthy glow!' Her pretty features became serious. 'Do watch your step with him, Jacqui.'

'Angela, really, you make it sound as if——'

'I know it's none of my business, but I've seen a few hearts broken over dear Dr Darling, and I think you wouldn't want to be hurt again so soon.'

'So soon?'

'Don't tell me you came to Maneroo just on a whim. There was a fellow behind it, wasn't there? Those first few weeks you were so close, so withdrawn sometimes.

You had to be getting over something, and it wasn't flu.'

'I suppose everybody's been speculating about me,' Jacqui said, piqued.

'No, only us more perceptive folk,' said Angela with a grin. She clapped a hand to her forehead. 'Now, what was I about to do? I know—Mr Johnson's X-rays. Suspected duodenal ulcer, remember? He had a barium meal yesterday. Dr Lambert's coming in to see him this afternoon. Will David be available if he wants to consult with him?'

Her earlier words had made Jacqui feel uncomfortably exposed. 'I really have no idea,' she said, a little more tersely than she intended. 'You'd better ask him.'

Angela, however, was not offended, and with a parting cheery remark she went off to the radiology department.

Nothing happened for a few days, and then just when Jacqui was beginning to wonder whether David had changed his mind about enlisting her help he rang through and asked her if she could spare him a few minutes before she went home.

It was remarkable, she thought, as she tapped on his door, that she had never been to his office before. It was at the other end of the building, on the ground floor. She'd simply never had any cause to go there to see him. To his abrupt, 'Come in!' she entered and found him standing at a light-table examining some X-rays. When he turned and smiled at her, Jacqui felt a weakening of her knees and that pleasant but alarming fluttering feeling inside that close proximity with David was always likely to trigger.

'Sorry to invade your spare time,' he said. 'Do sit down.'

Half an hour later she left his office with a commitment to attend a meeting of pro-Lakeside campaigners at the Swan Hotel at the weekend.

A week later she was in the thick of it all. David, as usual, was dotting 'i's and crossing 't's with the same fervour as he demonstrated in his hospital duties. Since the first meeting she had carefully studied the dossier she'd been given, which set out in detail the reasons why Maneroo should retain its hospital. At some time or another, David warned her, she was likely to be questioned by the Press. He was hoping for blanket media coverage locally, including debates on radio and television. There was a new public radio station willing to support the campaign, and he also hoped to organise a debate on the local television station, but as that broadcast from Hindmarsh, he could not, he told her, expect one hundred per cent support from them.

For the time being Jacqui's role was to sound out the opinions of patients and staff, and rally a group of nurses to help her organise the Open Day staff campaign. Staff would wear badges, erect banners and hand out leaflets to visitors. They would man a stall selling car stickers and badges proclaiming 'Maneroo needs Lakeside'. Jacqui was to organise the printing of T-shirts showing a cartoon of the hospital with further pithy slogans supporting its retention.

'I know someone in Melbourne whose brother does T-shirt printing,' Jacqui recalled. 'We might get a better price than in Hindmarsh, if I can twist his arm a little.'

David looked at her sharply. 'An old flame, eh?'

'No! Not at all. Just the brother of a friend.'

Jacqui managed to rearrange her shifts so that Li filled in for her while she made a lightning midweek trip to Melbourne. She alerted Lissa and was invited to stay at the flat.

'The air-bed is perishing waiting for you to come and visit us,' Lissa said, delighted at the unexpected return of her former flatmate.

'It'll be quicker if you fly,' David suggested when told of her plans. 'I'll fix it for you.'

'By balloon?' Jacqui joked, then wished she hadn't resurrected that memory. The expression that crossed David's face indicated that he hadn't forgotten that particular intimacy. She wondered briefly how it was between him and Rina Parkinson these days. She'd heard no rumours and was, anyway, quite determined not to become involved in the slightest with Dr Darling, no matter what his presence did to her pulse-rate.

'I wouldn't mind,' he said, a heart-melting half-smile curving his lips. 'But unfortunately that's not practicable. You'll have to go by regular air service. There's a daily commuter flight from Hindmarsh.'

He drove her to the airport at Hindmarsh and saw her on to the plane. 'Don't let the big city grab you back,' he said, as she was about to leave him. 'We need you here.' He clasped her firmly and impulsively crushed her lips with his. It was a brief, hard kiss, that might have been merely impersonal encouragement, but Jacqui could not fail to be aware of a passionate undertone. Maybe he just couldn't help it. 'Safe journey,' he said. 'Take care.'

She felt strangely bereft and lonely as she took her seat in the aircraft and looked out of the window. David saluted her gravely from the terminal building, and she waved, a lump in her throat as though she were going away forever.

From Melbourne airport she took a taxi to the flat that had been her home for nearly two years. She still had the key that Lissa had insisted she keep in case she ever arrived when Lissa was on duty, which was what the situation was now.

The flat looked much the same, except for Maggie's belongings now mingled with Lissa's. There was a huge felt-penned note on the kitchen table. 'Welcome. Help yourself to tucker. I got Bruce's phone number for you from Peggy so you could phone him straight away. See you this evening. Love, Lissa.'

The phone number of the T-shirt printer was scrawled across the bottom. Jacqui fixed herself a sandwich lunch and some coffee, then telephoned Bruce. No worries, he said, just come round and bring the artwork. He quoted her a very favourable price, and Jacqui felt pleased with this immediate success.

Straight after she'd eaten, she set off on her errand across Melbourne to the small printing business in Richmond where her former colleague's brother operated. The deal was settled quickly and Bruce promised delivery the following week.

As it was still early, Jacqui went into the city to browse around the shops. In the Bourke Street Mall she stood for a time listening to street musicians, then decided to go back to the flat and put her feet up for an hour. Tonight she would take Lissa and Maggie out to dinner in return for their putting her up for the night.

She was listening to a pair of young violinists earnestly playing 'The Flight of the Bumblebee' when a hand fell heavily on her shoulder. Startled, she jerked round and drew a sharp breath of dismay.

'Carey!'

'Hi, beautiful,' he said in the smooth, suave tone she remembered so well, the silkily persuasive voice whose deep tones had once set her nerve-ends tingling. It didn't now, she noted with slight surprise and considerable relief.

'Hello. . .' She was too taken aback to say anything more yet.

He hauled her out of the crowd to a more private spot. Holding her away from him, he studied her face. 'Just as lovely as ever. I've never known anyone with such gorgeous hair!' Her hair was loose and he toyed with it as though he still had a right to. Jacqui jerked away.

'How are—things?' she ventured, trying to avoid the light blue eyes that looked so innocent, yet masked a deviousness she had never suspected.

'Case comes up in a few days,' he said. 'I've got a good lawyer. I expect the charges to be dismissed.'

'Do you?' she said quietly, unable to bring herself to say she hoped so, or that that was good news.

'How about a drink?' he invited. 'And you can tell me what you're doing nowadays. You went up country, I heard.' He laughed. 'Didn't last long, did you? I could have told you so. You're a city slicker, Jacqui. When did you quit?'

'I haven't quit—I'm still there. I came down on business. I go back tomorrow.'

As they were talking he was urging her along, and it was a moment or two before Jacqui realised that she was letting him. She shook off the arm he'd laid casually across her shoulders.

'You'll have to excuse me, Carey,' she said, 'I've got a lot to do.'

'Didn't look like it a minute ago.' His confident smile irked her now. 'Come on, just for old times' sake. We're still friends, aren't we?'

Jacqui felt anger boiling up inside her. How could he be so casual, so nonchalant? 'No, I don't want to, Carey,' she said coldly. 'And we are certainly not still friends. You seem to have forgotten how you treated me. We were engaged, remember, and you were carrying on with another woman! You were about to break off our engagement, your mother told me. You didn't have the decency to tell *me* first! I had to find out myself!'

A tide of red briefly suffused his tanned face. 'Don't be bitter, Jacqui,' he said in a wheedling tone which made her flesh creep. 'Everyone makes a mistake some time in their lives, and Tania was mine.'

'You mean she's no consolation to you now?' Jacqui asked grimly.

'Tania? No fear. She dropped me like a hot brick as soon as she heard I'd been arrested.'

'Well, I can't say I blame her.'

He spread his hands wide. 'You women are all the same, condemning a man before he's even been before the court. I haven't done anything wrong.'

The carefree, charming Carey was still functioning, Jacqui thought. She couldn't even feel it in her heart to be sorry for him, guilty or not of the fraud charge. He had humiliated her, and that had hurt more than anything. Looking at him, she could only be glad she had escaped his particular brand of charisma. It was a timely reminder not to be fooled by anyone else.

'I'm sorry about that,' he said, blue eyes appealing

to her. 'I made a bit of a mess of things, but can't we talk it over in a civilised fashion? I've missed you, Jacqui.'

'No, Carey, there's nothing to talk over,' Jacqui said. Did he really imagine that all he had to do was apologise and she'd fall at his feet?

'My mother would love to see you,' he said persuasively.

Jacqui wouldn't have minded that, but she did not want to become involved again, even briefly, with Carey or his family. She shook her head. 'I'm sorry, Carey, there isn't time. I—er—I've got to go now, I'm meeting someone.'

He eyed her narrowly, hands shoved into the pockets of his expensive cord trousers, sleek suede jacket fitting smoothly across broad shoulders. He was good-looking, well-dressed, very personable. Yes, Jacqui thought, with the aid of a good lawyer, Carey will talk himself out of the mess he's in.

'A man, I suppose.'

'No.'

He looked sceptical but didn't press the point. He seemed to have accepted that she wasn't falling over herself to regain his attention. They said goodbye and she wished him luck in the court case. With relief she fled to the tram stop.

By the time Lissa came home, Jacqui had showered and changed and was watching television. She leapt up when she heard Lissa's key in the door, and they rushed into each other's arms.

'Jacqui! Fabulous!'

'Lissa! Great to see you.'

Lissa flung down her handbag. 'Gee, it feels as

though you've been away for years! Here, let's cele-
brate. Where's the sherry?'

'Where's Maggie?'

'She had to rush off home for a couple of days—her
mother's ill—so you can have her bed. She won't
mind.' Lissa slopped sherry into glasses and handed
one to Jacqui. 'Cheers!' She kicked her shoes across
the room and fell into a chair. 'What a day! I needed
you to cheer me up.'

'I thought we'd go out for a meal, if you're not too
exhausted. My treat.'

'Bless you, Jacqui. Just let me get rid of the taint of
vomit and disinfectant. I'm on Children's at the
moment and today they all decided to throw up on me.
No more blancmange for the little perishers unless I
make it myself. You should have seen the vile pink
stuff. Some of them chucked it at the walls, which I
have to admit was probably the most intelligent thing
to do with it. It's definitely improved the wallpaper!'

Jacqui laughed. Lissa's descriptions of nursing were
always colourful and hilarious. Lissa quaffed her sherry
and leapt up. 'I'll go and shower. Don't drink all the
sherry while I'm gone. We'll go to a BYO and we can
stop for a bottle of wine on the way.'

It was a cheerful evening. The two nurses caught up
on all the news over the meal and were still chatting
nineteen to the dozen when they arrived home. Lissa
had contrived to take the following day off, so there
was no rush to go to bed early, and they drank coffee
and continued talking until well after midnight.

'Tell me,' said Lissa at last, 'are there any dishy men
up in your neck of the woods? The scene's pretty grim
around here at the moment. All the best fellas are

married or living with someone. I'm beginning to feel like an outcast.'

Jacqui said carefully, 'Well, there's Dr Darling. Some people might think he was dishy.'

'Dr Darling? You're joking!'

'No—that's his name. You have to be careful not to pause after Doctor or it sounds provocative!'

'I love it,' said Lissa. 'Is he tall, dark and handsome?'

'Tall, fair and handsome.'

'Is he bespoke?'

'That's a little hard to tell. There does seem to be an on-off relationship going on, but he also has the reputation of being a bit of a flirt. He has a great deal of charm and sex appeal.' Making him sound so superficial was unfair, Jacqui knew, but she felt she couldn't tell Lissa what she really felt about David. She wasn't altogether sure what that was herself.

'Does he flirt with you?' Lissa gave her friend a sharply curious look.

'Don't worry, I'm not getting involved. Carey was lesson enough for me.' Jacqui hadn't yet mentioned her encounter with her former fiancé, but now she did.

'Ratbag,' said Lissa bluntly. 'In my opinion he deserves a long sentence.'

'He thinks he'll get off.'

Lissa snorted. 'He would! Well, I'm glad you're well away from it. Don't read the papers while the case is on, Jacqui. It'll only upset you.'

Jacqui's flight back to Hindmarsh was an afternoon one. David had promised to have someone meet her if he couldn't. As the plane came in to land Jacqui found herself hoping it would be Dr Darling awaiting her.

As Lissa was off duty the two girls had spent the

morning loafing around the flat, still talking, then had gone out for lunch, and finally Lissa had insisted on driving Jacqui to the airport. Apart from her encounter with Carey, it had been a pleasant two-day break, but once she was airborne Jacqui had discovered an eagerness to be back in Maneroo. She had no regrets about leaving the city again. Lissa had scoffed at the change in her, but Jacqui knew it was real. There was something about Maneroo and Lakeside Hospital that answered some need in her. That his name was Dr Darling, she was less willing to admit.

CHAPTER SEVEN

JACQUI felt a swift pang of disappointment when David was not at the Hindmarsh airport to meet her. Neither, it seemed, was anyone else. Her plane had been dead on time, so she decided to wait a while before phoning the hospital. David, or whoever else might be coming, might only have been slightly delayed. Perhaps David had had a phone call at the last minute or had had a problem finding someone else. . .

Her thoughts were broken off by a sudden confrontation with a man she had met several times casually on social occasions, Kirk Magnusson, owner of a string of country sports goods stores, and promoter of hot-air ballooning.

'Hello there,' he said, eyes flicking over her trim figure in white sleeveless top and brown cotton trousers. 'What are you doing here?' His approval was a little too obvious.

'Hello, Kirk. I've just got in from Melbourne. I was supposed to be met. . .' Jacqui glanced quickly at a group of people entering the arrivals area, but David was not among them, nor anyone she knew.

'I've just come from Mildura.' He treated her to an admiring look. 'I have the car here. I could give you a lift.'

'Thanks, but I'm sure someone's on the way.'

He didn't press the offer, but said, 'Well, what about a cup of coffee while we're waiting?'

'There's no need for you to——'

'Be gallant? Why not? It will be a pleasure.'

He already had a hand on her elbow and had picked up her overnight bag as he propelled her towards the refreshment counter. As it was in full view of the entrance, Jacqui did not argue. She was a little wary of Kirk Magnusson for the same reason she was wary of all good-looking men with charm. Like Carey, Kirk was a real smoothie. However, she let him buy her a coffee as it seemed he would be offended if she refused.

'You haven't been ballooning with David again,' he observed, eyes keenly on her face.

'No, I haven't.'

His smile was flattering. 'I've seen you at the tennis club. You have a nice style. We must have a game some time.'

'I'm not very good.' She had watched Kirk play and knew he was expert.

'What else do you do with your off duty?' he queried with an arched eyebrow. 'Maneroo's not exactly a centre of exciting activities.'

'I find plenty to occupy me. I swim quite a lot, and I sometimes lend a hand at the youth club. We're a bit like a family at the hospital, so there's often a birthday party or barbecue to go to.'

'Isn't the pace a little slow for a sophisticated city girl?' he suggested.

Jacqui had never thought of herself as sophisticated. 'I seem to be busy enough.'

'You must miss the variety of entertainment the city offers, though. I know I'd go mad if I didn't get away regularly.'

Jacqui said truthfully, 'A change is as good as a holiday, they say.'

He tempted, 'Hindmarsh has quite a good repertory theatre. Have you been to any of their shows?'

'I've seen their posters in Maneroo, but no, I haven't.' She guessed what might be coming next, and wasn't sure if she welcomed it or not.

'I'm a subscriber, so what about coming with me to a show some time?' Kirk invited. 'We could have dinner first. There are one or two rather more up-market restaurants in Hindmarsh. Next Saturday night, maybe?'

Jacqui was almost going to pretend she was doing something on Saturday, until it suddenly struck her that going out with Kirk Magnusson might be good for her. Lately, she was thinking about David rather more than was wise. Kirk, good-looking, debonair and easy-going company could be just the diversion she needed. There was no danger, she told herself, that she would find her blood running hot in his company. She was not in the least attracted to him, but as an alternative to David he might be an effective temporary prescription for her.

'Thanks, that would be nice,' she answered. 'They're doing *My Fair Lady*, aren't they? I never did see it on stage.'

He looked pleased. 'I'll pick you up about five. That should give us plenty of time to drive in and have dinner before the show starts. You're in the flat in Batman Street?'

Jacqui nodded. Before she could say anything else, she caught sight of a rather agitated David bursting through the entrance doors. She stood up. 'Here's David. Thanks for the coffee, Kirk.' Hurriedly she picked up her bag and started towards Dr Darling just as he switched his gaze to the refreshment counter. He looked relieved at the sight of her.

'Jacqui, I'm sorry I'm late. There was an accident on the road and I had to stop. An ambulance wasn't required, fortunately, only minor medical treatment.' Then he realised who she was with. 'Oh, hello, Kirk.' His tone cooled noticeably.

Kirk said, 'I would have given Jacqui a lift, if necessary.'

Jacqui thanked him again, and was glad he didn't make a parting remark about seeing her on Saturday, though it couldn't possibly matter if David knew she was going out with him. They parted outside the terminal building and Jacqui got into David's car.

He looked at her for a long moment. 'You look cheerful. You must have had a good time?' He sounded a shade resentful.

'Brief but enjoyable. My erstwhile flatmate and I chewed the rag until all hours.'

The big green car swung away from the airport. 'She didn't persuade you to go back to the SCG?'

'She didn't try. I wouldn't want to renege on my agreement with Lakeside anyway.'

'No, but afterwards. . .'

She was puzzled at his attitude. 'You harp on the fact that I'm a city girl so much I'm beginning to think you're trying to drive me back!'

He laughed. 'Or goad you into staying just to make me a liar!'

Jacqui said, 'It can't really make much difference to you whether I stay or not.'

He negotiated a bend, then glanced at her briefly before saying, 'I don't like the hospital losing good nurses.'

Well, she'd asked for that. She'd hardly expected him to say he had personal reasons for wanting her to stay.

'I ordered the T-shirts,' she told him. 'They'll be here in a week.'

'I've got our local jobbing printer doing the stickers and posters. He's on our side and is doing them free.'

'Fantastic. I couldn't persuade Bruce to do that, but I did wangle a ten-per-cent discount,' Jacqui reported.

'Good work!'

They talked about the campaign, then got on to what had been happening on her ward during the past two days.

David was candid. 'Li's very conscientious, but she doesn't have your flair.'

Jacqui dismissed the compliment lightly, but felt warmed by it. Or was David just flattering her because he wanted to persuade her to stay on at Lakeside and take over Greta's job?

When he dropped her off at her flat, she felt obliged to offer him coffee, but he declined, saying he had to get back to the hospital, and he was sure she must be tired anyway. There was to be a campaign meeting the following Monday evening, he told her. Then, to her surprise, he said,

'Feel like going ballooning again this weekend? I should be able to get away on Sunday.'

Jacqui said truthfully, 'I'm sorry, but I'm going to a barbecue lunch with the youth club on Sunday. Angela and I are both invited.'

'I could get you back by lunchtime.'

It wasn't easy to say no. This time there would almost certainly be passengers, but she wasn't going to be David Darling's 'second string', his refuge from a stormy relationship with Rina. 'I'd rather not,' she said firmly. 'Just in case something unforeseen made us late back.'

He knew she was making an excuse. 'Oh well, some other time, then.'

'Thanks, anyway.' She suddenly wished she hadn't said no. Don't be a fool! snapped her common sense immediately.

She watched him drive off with a hollow feeling inside. It was crazy, of course, to feel disappointed. It would have been even crazier to go ballooning again!

When Saturday arrived, Jacqui was not at all certain she wanted to go to the theatre and have dinner with Kirk. However, by the time he called for her, she had convinced herself that going out with other men was the best way to avoid the trap of falling in love with David Darling. She wore a neat black and white dress and jacket and put her hair up into a softer chignon than the one she wore for work.

Kirk arrived punctually. Talking to him on the journey to Hindmarsh, Jacqui learned that he had been an Olympic oarsman and had lived in England for a couple of years. He knew London well, so that proved a major topic of conversation. He also talked about the potential of Maneroo for water-sports and the benefits of the proposed tourist complex to the town. He showed polite interest in her, her family and her career, and by the time they reached the larger town Jacqui felt more at ease with him, but had marked him down as one Maneroo resident who would not join the campaign against the closure of Lakeside.

He took her to a very pleasant restaurant, and over the meal the conversation suddenly turned to the hospital and its future. Kirk confirmed her earlier opinion of his view of the matter.

'A lot of people don't want it to close,' Jacqui remarked. She was careful not to be too specific as David had told her to keep their plans under her hat for the time being.

Kirk said, 'The whole thing is cut and dried. The council only has to ratify the decision and the developers will start work. There's no other site they're willing to consider, and if they don't get it they'll go elsewhere. Which would be a pity for Maneroo.'

'But Lakeside can't close down until the new Hindmarsh hospital is complete,' Jacqui reminded him. She didn't tell him what David had said about an alternative site becoming available.

'It can be wound down,' Kirk said confidently. 'Demolition might have to be delayed a little, but I think Hindmarsh will be completed fairly soon. They've just received substantial Government funding.' He looked around for the waiter and asked for the bill. 'We'd better be getting along,' he said to Jacqui.

They had excellent seats at the theatre and the show was well done. To Jacqui's embarrassment she fell asleep on the way home and didn't wake until they were driving along the main street of Maneroo.

'Oh, dear, I am sorry. . .' she apologised. 'That was very rude of me.'

'You nurses do a very tiring job,' Kirk said gallantly. He parked outside the house and turned to her with a smile. 'I enjoyed your company anyway! We must do it again some time.'

'Yes. Thank you for a very pleasant evening, Kirk.'

He got out and saw her to her door, where she

thanked him again and he said he hoped he would see her soon at the tennis club. She didn't invite him in for coffee, although she felt a little ungrateful not doing so, but she didn't want to give any wrong impressions. It had been a pleasant evening out, she thought later, lying in bed, but she wasn't sure if she really wanted to go out with Kirk again.

'I hope you enjoyed your lunch party yesterday.' David Darling's voice was pleasantly conversational, and his remark casual. In fact he almost sounded as though he was interested!

'It was fun.' There was no reason for Jacqui to flush guiltily, as though she had manufactured an excuse not to go ballooning with him. She had, after all, gone to the party, and if he didn't believe her he could ask Angela. Or was it really Saturday night she felt guilty about because she hadn't mentioned it? Well, that was just plain ridiculous. She didn't have to tell Dr Darling everywhere she was going. Even if someone from Maneroo had seen her with Kirk and mentioned it, it was no business of his. It was just her idiotic imagination suggesting that his tone was faintly suspicious. He couldn't care what she did, for goodness' sake.

'You haven't forgotten tonight's meeting?' he asked her.

'No.'

He was lounging in the doorway to her office, having just arrived for the morning round. Jacqui wished he weren't quite so handsome, and that he didn't have such penetrating dark eyes. It was always a temptation to imagine he was thinking thoughts he undoubtedly was not and that the look was specially for her, even though she knew he probably looked at all women that way. It was all part of his masculine sex appeal. Which he possessed a little too much of, she thought, dragging her reluctant eyes away from the man who tormented her emotionally more than any man she had ever known.

'We hope to get down to brass tacks tonight,' he told her.

'Where is the meeting?' Jacqui asked, realising he hadn't mentioned that important fact. 'At the Swan again?'

He looked surprised. 'At my place—my parents' house. You know where it is?'

'No. . .should I?'

'Lorrimer Street, number ten. You'll see the surgery sign outside.'

Jacqui gave a teasing smile. 'I wonder what your parents would think of your using their house for subversive activities!'

He laughed. 'My father has been conducting subversive activities amongst the hierarchy of the medical profession for most of his life, and my mother, had she been born at the right time, would have been a suffragette. As it is she's a fairly militant fund-raiser for good causes, and sometimes lost ones. I come from a long line of radicals.'

'So it's a hereditary disease.'

He took a step inside her office. 'Is that all you think it is?' A slightly hurt look had shadowed his eyes and Jacqui regretted what had only been a teasing remark.

'No, of course I don't. I know you're absolutely sincere,' she said, getting up. It surprised her how sensitive he could be sometimes. 'Shall we start now?' she asked, referring to the round he had come to do.

They went out together, and by the time they

reached the first patient the professional had overlaid the personal relationship.

'I've got good news for you,' David told Mrs Reilly, an elderly diabetic patient. 'You can go home tomorrow. But. . .' he shook a finger half seriously at her '. . .you must promise me, and Dr Prentiss, that you'll stick to the diet and never miss your insulin. It doesn't matter if you do feel well. It's only by sticking to doctor's orders, to the letter, that you'll go on feeling well. If you look after yourself, I reckon there's another couple of decades left in you, diabetes or not.'

Mrs Reilly rolled her eyes and said to Jacqui, 'I hope he doesn't lecture you nurses the way he goes on at patients.'

Jacqui answered with a straight face, 'He does, Mrs Reilly. We have to watch our "p"s and "q"s too, you know. But Dr Darling knows what he's talking about. We don't want you being brought in here in a coma again, do we?'

'Thank you, Sister,' said David, with a wink at her.

Mrs Reilly cackled appreciatively. She did a spot of finger-wagging herself. 'I'll have you know, Doctor, if I live another two decades I'll be ninety-eight!'

'I never would have guessed,' David flattered, although he knew perfectly well how old she was. 'And if you can still get your sums right you must be good for years yet.'

'I can't work those new-fangled calculators,' Mrs Reilly complained. 'I still add up in my head and I get the right answer just as quick, what's more.' She added proudly, 'Jed, my grandson, says he'd rather have me doing the accounts for the nursery than any young 'un.'

'I don't blame him. Would you like Sister to ring him and ask him to come and fetch you home tomorrow?'

Mrs Reilly shook her head independently. 'I'll do it myself. Sister's got more than enough to do running around after old nuisances like me, and young nuisances like you!' She cackled again, appreciating her own wit. Then gravely she said, 'I want to thank you, Doctor, for all you've done. And don't worry, I won't be back.' The irrepressible smile broke through. 'I couldn't stand another one of your lectures!' She offered them both a barley sugar from the bag on her bedside table, but, catching David's eye, did not take one herself.

When they had seen the other two patients in Mrs Reilly's ward and were out in the corridor again, Jacqui said, 'She's a character, isn't she? Mrs Reilly, I mean. If it weren't for the Australian accent, I could believe she was pure cockney.'

'It's quite likely her forebears were,' David suggested. 'She's a Blessington, and the Blessingtons are an old pioneer family around here. Been here since gold rush days at least. Likewise the Reillys. Martha's husband was a farmer and haulier, huge man, drank a lot, but was never violent. They had twelve children, all girls. Poor George desperately wanted a son.'

'I guess you'd have to give them marks for trying,' said Jacqui drily. She was touched by the affectionate tone David used. She had noticed it often. It wasn't an assumed bedside manner, it was simply that he liked and respected and genuinely cared about the people he treated. His charm was more than skin-deep.

The day went quickly as always, but it was quieter than usual. There were empty beds in the ward, and no new admissions. Jacqui was able to direct her nurses to do routine jobs that tended to get neglected when the pace was hectic, and she was able to catch up on the paperwork that seemed never-ending.

'It's as bad as the NHS,' she complained to Angela, who laughed. She had brought Jacqui a mid-afternoon cup of tea and biscuits and stopped for a chat.

'Longing to get back to it?' Angela asked.

'Oddly enough, no. Though everyone seems to expect me to be, and treats me as though I might sprout wings and fly off and leave them in the lurch any minute.'

'Maybe you'll settle in Australia like me,' Angela suggested. She added slyly, 'Maybe if you meet the right man. . .'

'Oh, I'm not ready for that kind of settling down,' Jacqui declared. 'But I am getting rather attached to country living. I like the friendliness and the slower pace. We're busy but not quite so rushed off our feet all the time. I have time to stop and contemplate the lake! Or catch up with the paperwork.'

'I've never known it so quiet,' Angela said reflectively. 'I hope it's not the calm before the epidemic!'

'So do I!' Jacqui glanced out of the window. 'Maybe the hot weather has something to do with it.'

Angela crossed to the window and looked down towards the lake. 'There's a brisk north-easterly today. I dare say we'll have a windsurfer or two with sprained ankles or concussion.' She came back to Jacqui. 'Is it right that David's spearheading a move to gain support for keeping Lakeside open?'

Jacqui avoided a direct answer. 'Who told you that?'

Angela looked at her closely. 'The rumour's been floating around the hospital for a couple of days. I got the impression you were enlisted. If so, count me in. I'll be glad to help in any way I can. I don't want the place to close, and I know a lot of people here feel the same, but no one's actually spoken up about it. They need to be mobilised.'

Jacqui felt bound to come clean. 'That's precisely what David says. He's been keeping a low profile so as not to give the other side time to set up their own campaign propaganda. I don't think they realise how much opposition to the closure there is. He's about to launch the attack this week with full media coverage. There's a meeting tonight, as a matter of fact, to discuss the campaign. I'm going to be involved in organising all staff who are in favour of us staying open for business, and who want to help, on Open Day. So be prepared. We've got to make a big impact then.'

'Well, I'm glad someone's had the guts to oppose the closure,' Angela said. 'And I'm glad it's David. If anyone can turn the tide, he can.'

There were a dozen people at David's house that night, some of whom Jacqui had not met before. David chaired the meeting and for a while there was brisk discussion, some mild argument, but plenty of solidarity.

At ten forty-five, David declared the meeting closed and offered everyone tea or coffee.

'Want to give me a hand?' he asked Jacqui.

She jumped up and followed him into the kitchen, fetching cups and saucers from the cupboard he indicated while he put the kettle on to boil.

'Any biscuits or cake?' she asked.

'Try that big tin with the roses on. I think there are some left.'

Jacqui opened it. 'Maybe one each! Why didn't you tell me? I could have brought something for supper.'

'Never crossed my mind,' he said, grinning at her.

'Men!'

'You wouldn't want to be without us!' Passing her, he brushed his lips across her cheek and she drew back, startled. He was in an ebullient mood because of the success of the meeting.

'It was a terrific meeting,' she said. 'You've picked good helpers.' She said it without thinking that she was including herself.

David came up behind her and massaged her shoulders lightly, laying his cheek against her hair. 'Especially this one,' he said softly.

'Now you're flirting with me.'

'Do you mind?'

The deep probing of his fingers in her tired shoulders was soothing, and his nearness was heating her blood alarmingly. It was just as well the kettle boiled at that point and excused her from having to answer with a lie.

People lingered for another hour, talking, and there was a definite air of confidence among them that heartened Jacqui. Although she'd agreed to help, she'd feared that it was, as Kirk had said, probably a lost cause. When bureaucrats decided to do things, it was usually well-nigh impossible to change their course. She had to admire David for taking on the council, and tonight she had begun to feel that he might indeed win.

She got up to go when the rest of them did, but David whispered in her ear, 'Aren't you going to help me wash the cups?'

She should have made an excuse, but instead she began collecting the cups and saucers, and while David said goodnight to the rest of the volunteers she piled the crockery on a tray and carried it out to the kitchen.

She was running hot water in the sink when he reappeared.

'Here. . .you need this.' He slipped an apron around her and tied the strings, letting his hands linger briefly on her slender waist. Jacqui concentrated on the cups she was washing and tried to ignore the sparks flying between them.

David grabbed a towel off a rail and wiped up, whistling cheerily. He was obviously well pleased with the outcome of the evening. It was only after she had let the water out of the sink that she saw the dishwasher.

'You didn't tell me you had a dishwasher,' she accused, glaring at him. 'You didn't need me to wash up for you.'

'I quite forgot,' he said nonchalantly. 'I was so busy thinking how nice you'd look in my mother's frilly aprons!'

'Idiot!' Jacqui pulled open the door of the dishwasher and gasped. It was chock-a-block with dirty china and pots. 'David Darling, how long is it since you ran this?'

He shrugged and mumbled, 'I don't know. A few days, maybe. I'm not here all that often. It seems pointless to run it for a couple of things. Uneconomic and environmentally irresponsible,' he finished complacently.

'You are the limit. Well, I'm going to run it for you now.' She repacked the machine more tidily and with less risk to the crockery, closed the door and fiddled with the dials. 'Now I'm going home. Don't forget to empty it, will you?'

He flung the teatowel over the rail, and raced after her. 'Jacqui, don't go for a minute. . .let's have another cup of coffee?'

A lock of tawny blond hair dipped over his forehead, making Jacqui's fingers itch to smooth it back into place. She controlled the urge and said, 'No, thanks. It's too late. I won't sleep.'

With an arm stretched across the doorway, he barred her way into the living-room where she'd left her handbag. 'A nightcap, then. Something to make you sleep like a top. There are a couple more things I want to discuss with you.'

Jacqui doubted that, but she felt herself weakening anyway.

'We both need to unwind a little,' he murmured persuasively. 'After a hard day and a fairly tense evening.'

'I had a very quiet day,' she said, 'and I thought this evening was quite stimulating.'

'God damn it, woman, do you have to be so perverse?' he exploded.

Jacqui laughed. 'All right, just a quick one. Then I really must go.'

He gave her a victory smile, lowered his arm and allowed her to go into the living-room. She sank on to the big comfortable sofa while he opened a drinks cabinet.

'Brandy or whisky?' he asked.

'Brandy, thanks.'

'And dry?'

'Lovely.'

While he poured the drinks, there was silence, broken only by the sound of ice chinking into their glasses. Jacqui looked around the room, seeing it properly for the first time. It was a big old high-ceilinged drawing-room with ornate cornices and a centre rose, a huge slate fireplace and heavy Victorian dark oak furniture. But it was comfortable and plainly well lived-in, a real family room.

'Lovely old house,' she remarked, as David handed her her drink.

He sat beside her. 'Yes, it is. A bit ramshackle now. Dad's always saying he must get things done to it, but he never does. It'll fall down around their ears first. The garden's enormous and like a jungle. You'll have to see it in daylight.'

'Do you have brothers and sisters?'

'Yes. My brother's a surgeon in Sydney and my sister's a speech therapist, married to an architect in Perth. There were half a dozen nieces and nephews at the last count.'

'Well, here's to the success of Operation Lakeside,' Jacqui said, raising her glass.

David clinked his glass against hers. 'And to you. Thanks for helping, Jacqui.'

'I haven't done anything yet,' she protested.

'You will. I have every confidence in your ability, Sister Brent.' He downed half his drink and looked steadily at her. 'You're a first-rate nurse, Jacqui. I'm sorry if I gave the impression when you first arrived that I thought you might be the flighty type, using your profession to get a free return air ticket, and that Maneroo was just another convenient stopover on your sightseeing trip around Australia.'

'You don't have to keep apologising.'

'I get the feeling, though, that you're still prickly with me. Does it still niggle that I once called you a city slicker?'

She laughed. 'I'm used to colourful language! No, David, it doesn't niggle. At first I was annoyed, but in fact I wasn't sure myself that you're weren't right.'

He didn't continue that topic, but finished his drink and put the glass on the table. 'You know what I'm going to do?' A slightly mischievous smile played about his mouth and, before Jacqui could prevent him, he had leaned across and loosened the clasp that secured her plait to the top of her head. The thick glossy braid fell to her shoulder.

'Hey, what are you doing?'

'Letting your hair down,' he murmured, and deftly removed the band from the end of the plait. 'You look much too severe with it up.'

Why she didn't just leap up and tell him not to be an idiot, Jacqui never knew, but she sat there as though hypnotised while he unbraided her hair and ran his fingers through the silky waves which sprang in little copper curls around them.

'I thought you said you had a few more things to tell me,' she said in a wobbly tone.

His fingers massaged her scalp, and he smiled. 'I only wanted to tell you how beautiful and desirable you are. . .'

She was somewhere else when he took the glass from her fingers and put it beside his on the table. And she was still in this Cloud-cuckoo-land when his warm lips touched hers, tentatively caressing at first, then with mounting passion.

'Jacqui. . .' With a little sigh, he pushed her gently down on the couch, pulling a cushion under her head, stretching his body alongside hers, and the terrible part was that she let him do it. She seemed to have no will-power, only an overpowering need to be in his arms, to feel him close.

There was a deep and satisfying pleasure when his hand slid under her blouse and his fingers curved over her breast as his lips claimed hers again. There was a delicious sensation of warmth coiling through her, probing emotional depths whose existence had been unknown to her before. It was the kind of thing that only happened when you were in love, she thought, pulling his head closer to deepen their kiss as she pressed herself more intimately against his own demanding body.

The insistent electronic summons of the telephone went unanswered for long moments, until at last it penetrated both their consciousnesses. David rolled reluctantly off the couch. 'This ought not to happen in real life! I'd better answer it.'

He was gone just long enough for Jacqui to straighten her blouse and rake her hair back off her face. She was reaching for her handbag and about to stand up when David came in. He said exactly what she had expected.

'I've got to go. There's a cardiac arrest on the way by ambulance.'

Jacqui smiled at him. 'I guessed as much.'

He came to her, held her briefly. 'Sometimes I wish I weren't a doctor!'

More for her own ears than his, she said drily, 'Maybe it's just as well you are.'

CHAPTER EIGHT

JACQUI did not see very much of the coronary patient who had been rushed in the previous night. Soon after her arrival next morning, he was transferred to Melbourne by air ambulance. There was no separate coronary care unit at Lakeside, so he had been specialled in the ICU overnight. Medical's night staff all looked a bit frazzled, and David, Jacqui saw with concern, was obviously nearly dead on his feet. He was still with the patient when she took over from the night sister and went into the ward to see if she could give any assistance. He looked at her with a weary smile.

'Good morning,' she murmured quietly. 'How is he?'

'Holding his own. Thank God for defibrillators and anti-clotting drugs. We're moving him to Melbourne as soon as the 'copter arrives.'

'Yes, I know. Is there anything you want me to do now?'

He shook his head. 'You can give me a hand when they put him on the stretcher. There'll be a nurse with them, so no one will need to go from here.'

Jacqui ran her eyes over the patient. 'Is it his first?'

David nodded. 'Yes.'

'How bad is he?'

'Judging by the ECG, pretty bad. My guess is they'll decide to do a bypass.'

'And head him in the right direction diet-wise, I hope. He looks overweight.'

'Very. And a smoker too. Not to mention the booze.

134

I know Alan Fowler slightly, and he had it coming. The only exercise he ever does is to put his hand in his pocket for the money for the next drink or packet of fags.'

By nine o'clock the air ambulance had been and gone. There had been a small flurry of curiosity among staff and patients at the arrival of the helicopter on the hospital lawn, and while the patient was being trans-ferred with infinite care from the ward to its interior. The nurse who had come with the ambulance was experienced in cardiac emergencies. Jacqui was impressed with the sophisticated life-support equip-ment aboard the helicopter.

Seeing that Matron Wallace was talking to David afterwards, Jacqui walked back to her ward alone. To her surprise, a few minutes later, David appeared.

'You're not going to do the rounds today,' Jacqui told him severely. 'You're all in. I suppose you've been up all night?'

'More or less.' He sagged into a chair. 'I'm all right.'

'You're not. Go and get some sleep. We can send for you if we need you. Things are pretty quiet right now and there isn't anyone you really need to see urgently.' He looked stubborn, so she said, 'Please, David. . .You're overdoing it. You'll be ill yourself if you're not careful.'

'I was just thinking,' he muttered, resting his chin on clasped hands, 'that we really do need a modern comprehensive coronary care unit here. Alan Fowler's the umpteenth patient we've had to airlift to Melbourne this year. If we could avoid moving some patients for whom major surgery isn't appropriate. . .'

'Surely Hindmarsh's new hospital will have one?' she reminded him with a sly smile.

'But they won't have their own air ambulance,' he said, 'and road transport can be life-threatening, as well as too slow. Alan will be tucked up in the Alfred almost as soon as we could get him to Hindmarsh. I don't envisage us doing major surgery, but. . .' His voice slurred slightly and one elbow slid off the arm of the chair. His body jerked as tiredness almost overcame him.

'David!' said Jacqui severely. 'Go and get some sleep. Now's not the time to start taking on new causes! Save Lakeside first, then think about your next project! Meanwhile, you need a few hours' rest. Don't be so pig-headed about it.'

He looked up and grinned faintly. 'You're taking a bit of a liberty, aren't you, Sister, giving orders to medical staff?'

'If you don't go, I'll fetch Matron,' she threatened, trying to drag him out of the chair.

That made him rise. He yawned and dragged the back of his hand across his forehead. 'OK, I'm going.' She was close enough for him to throw an arm around her shoulders and rest his forehead briefly on her shoulder. Then he raised it and, so quickly she was taken by surprise, kissed her, his mouth clinging to hers as though he'd been long deprived.

Jacqui shunted him to the door. 'You're too tired to know what you're doing. Off you go.' She knew he would not go home, but would snatch a few hours' sleep in his office suite, which included a bedroom, as well as kitchen and bathroom. Had he not been a local, with existing accommodation in the town, he would have lived permanently at the hospital.

When he had gone, Jacqui closed her door and spent a few minutes composing herself. It was ridiculous the way the man could scatter her wits and reach to her innermost emotions at the drop of a hat. She really must pull herself together. More sport, she prescribed for herself, more tennis and swimming, maybe even squash, but definitely no ballooning!

With the longer evenings that came with the change to daylight saving, Jacqui sometimes managed a game of tennis on a week night, or went for a swim at the local Olympic pool. Kirk Magnusson played tennis regularly, and since their date in Hindmarsh they often had a game together, or joined others in doubles matches. She had also been out with him again once or twice, to dinner and on a sightseeing drive to the Grampians. He had suggested a weekend in Melbourne a couple of times, and had invited her to go to the Melbourne Cup horse-race with him, but Jacqui had politely declined.

David also turned up occasionally at tennis, and Jacqui always felt that he looked a little askance at her if Kirk was around. He didn't seem to like the man much. Since the night she had stayed after the campaign meeting and their lovemaking had been interrupted, she had been careful not to be alone with David and he had not contrived to arrange it. Maybe, she thought, things were going smoothly with Rina again.

Jacqui saw Rina Parkinson a couple of times at the tennis club, but no one introduced them. Eventually she met her in a rather unexpected way. She had been shopping in Maneroo one Saturday morning and had stopped for a cup of coffee in a rather pleasant little coffee lounge that she often went to. She had scarcely sat down at a table when she was joined by Rina. At first Jacqui thought it was just a coincidence, but Rina evidently knew who she was and had come to her table purposely.

'You're Jacqui Brent, aren't you?' Close up the girl was even slimmer than Jacqui remembered. Her ivory skin and dark hair made her eyes seem enormous, and her mouth was a scarlet slash that emphasised rather too prominent cheekbones. She looked anorexic to Jacqui. The dark smudges under her eyes that showed through her make-up were unhealthy and the veins stood out in the almost transparent skin on the backs of her small delicate hands which she moved restlessly on the table.

'Yes, I am,' said Jacqui.

'I'm Rina Parkinson.'

'Yes, I know. Hello.'

The girl seemed surprised that Jacqui knew her, but Jacqui did not bother to give any explanation since one was not sought.

'I've seen you at the tennis club,' Rina said.

The waitress hovered, waiting for an order, and Jacqui invited the other girl to have a coffee. Rina thanked her offhandedly.

'You're only at the hospital temporarily, aren't you?' asked Rina, giving Jacqui a thorough examination from under slightly lowered lashes.

'I'm filling in for Sister Martin until she gets back from her long service leave, which will be in a few weeks' time. After that I may take over from Sister Hermann who's leaving to have a baby.'

'I heard you were helping David with the campaign to stop the hospital being closed.' Rina's mouth tightened a little.

'I'm trying to.' It was no secret now. The media had

begun reporting the views of people like David, and interest was gradually building up.

'I don't know why he didn't ask me to help,' Rina complained. 'What can it matter to you whether Lakeside survives or not? You don't intend to live here for good, do you?' She looked belligerent, as though Jacqui had no right even to consider it.

'There seem to be compelling reasons why Lakeside shouldn't be closed,' Jacqui said, 'so I'm happy to help. And I suppose David asked me to simply because I'm a senior nurse at Lakeside. The whole hospital is involved, however. I'm just co-ordinating activities there.'

Rina seemed not wholly convinced. 'Do you like David?' she asked.

'Yes. He's a very fine doctor.' Rina was very young, Jacqui realised now she was only across the table from her. The girl she had supposed in the dim light at Mario's and in the distance at the tennis club to be twenty-two or -three was probably, in fact, no more than eighteen or nineteen.

'I meant do you like him—in a sexual way?' Rina asked candidly.

Taken by surprise, Jacqui felt herself blushing. 'He's a very attractive man,' she said, 'but if you're suggesting there's anything between us——' She broke off as their coffee arrived, and it was Rina who took up the conversation.

'I think you ought to know that we're practically engaged.'

'I was aware that there was a—a relationship,' Jacqui said. 'You can't keep secrets in a small town, I've discovered.'

'It's no secret that David and I are in love,' said

Rina, with a faintly triumphant smile. 'I don't mind who knows it.'

'You'll be getting engaged soon?' Jacqui prompted, wondering how she had got involved in such a conversation. And wondering too what David could possibly see in this rather vapid little girl. She was very attractive in a gamine kind of way, but jealousy was giving her a hard expression at the moment. Laughably, she seemed to see Jacqui as a rival.

'Not formally. David and I don't believe in marriage. We intend to live together. I—I haven't been too well lately, but I'm better now, so David can stop being impatient. As soon as our parents return from overseas, we'll be moving into a place of our own.' Rina gave a husky laugh and directed a meaningful look at Jacqui. 'I hope you haven't been getting any ideas about him. The nurses do, you know, because he's so handsome and sexy, and he flirts with them a bit. It doesn't mean anything, though. I thought I'd better tell you that so you won't get hurt.'

Jacqui was amazed at the girl's blatant hypocrisy. You don't give a dman whether I get hurt or not, she thought, you're just warning me off. She decided she'd had enough conversation with Rina Parkinson. She finished her coffee, then slung her bag over her shoulder and picked up her carrier bag of shopping. 'I'm afraid I've got to go. Nice meeting you, Rina.' And as she marched out of the coffee shop, Jacqui found she was seething more at David than his girlfriend.

If the likes of Rina Parkinson were what David Darling fancied, then he was welcome to her. So he didn't believe in marriage. Well, if Rina was prepared to live with him without a marriage certificate, and put up with his almost certain infidelities, then that was her affair. She might be bowled over by Dr Darling's brand of charisma, but Jacqui Brent certainly was not. The tight feeling in her chest was anger, nothing else.

She had lunch alone, did some laundry and then decided to spend the rest of the day writing letters. She had been intending to play tennis, but Kirk would probably be there, and suddenly she didn't feel in the mood for Kirk's flattery and attention. There was a tennis club dance that night, but she decided to give that a miss too.

She had just screwed up her first attempt at a letter to Lissa because it seemed to reflect her edgy mood, although she hadn't even mentioned David Darling, when the telephone pierced the silence of the empty flat.

Kirk, she guessed, to ask if she was playing tennis today, and going to the club dance that evening. She was half inclined not to answer it, but ringing telephones were hard to ignore. Her guess was wrong. It was Jennie Morris, who was on nights. She had wrenched her ankle and didn't think she could manage to go in that night. Jacqui agreed it would be unwise, told her to rest her leg and not to worry, that she'd do the night shift herself.

Jennie was grateful, insisted that her ankle was not sprained and she would be able to do her shift the following night. 'You won't have to break a date, I hope,' she said anxiously.

'Not tonight,' said Jacqui, glad of the excuse in case Kirk should ring.

Working would give her something to do, she reflected later. It would help to keep her mind from wild surmises about David and Rina Parkinson. It annoyed her greatly that she couldn't seem to keep her thoughts permanently away from conjecturing about them. It was hardly surprising, she conceded finally, that David was enamoured of the dark-haired girl. With a little more flesh on her bones, Rina would be quite beautiful. Maturity would probably see to that. He must be nearly twice her age, but age differences didn't really matter if people loved each other. Did David love Rina? Or was he taking advantage of her because she was young and beautiful and crazy about him?

Jacqui managed to snatch a couple of hours' sleep that afternoon, so she felt refreshed and rested when she reported for night duty. It was quite a while since Jacqui had done a night shift. She had almost forgotten how different a hospital could be at night, when all the hustle and bustle of the daytime routine was out of the way and only a skeleton staff were on duty. There were still only a few patients in the medical ward, and several of them were on the point of being discharged, so there was not likely to be a great deal to do unless there was an emergency.

Jacqui was alone except for a young nursing aide, who was taking the opportunity of night duty with little to do to continue studying. So in the end Jacqui found that her mind had no more to occupy it than if she'd been at home. At least there she would have been watching television as a distraction. She took the opportunity to file some case notes and write up some reports, but there wasn't enough to occupy the whole shift. She watched a little television in the patients' day lounge, but there was nothing very interesting on, so she stopped to chat for a while to one insomniac who was in a room by himself.

She made him a warm drink, listened to the story of

his life, gave him a sedative, and when he had dropped off to sleep she went back to her office, wishing she didn't feel so bleak. She wondered if David was out with Rina somewhere tonight, and rebuked herself for wishing there would be an emergency to interrupt their intimacy the way it had happened with her.

'What's come over you?' she whispered into the emptiness of her office, filled with shame. 'That's a terrible thought.'

The night dragged slowly. Jacqui found herself glancing at her watch innumerable times. There were few patient calls, and when she did her rounds at the appointed intervals all was quiet and calm. It was eerie being awake in a place where everyone else was sleeping, and the lighting outside the wards was low.

At two a.m. Sally, the aide, made tea and brought a cup for Jacqui. They chatted for a while about Sally's studies, about the patients, the hospital and the campaign to save it, then Sally went back to her reading. Less than half an hour had passed, and Jacqui contemplated the hours till dawn and the first shift's arrival gloomily. She also contemplated Sunday which, despite the fact that she would sleep most of the morning, yawned ahead like an abyss. In fact, in the small quiet hours when thoughts seemed to assume exaggerated proportions, her entire future seemed a formless void.

When Jacqui returned from her last round before breakfast, satisfied that all was quiet and peaceful, dawn was just breaking. She looked out over the lake, grey and still but beginning to reflect the pink-tinged sky. A duck rose suddenly from the reeds along the shoreline, probably honking loudly, but the sound was inaudible to her, a couple of hundred metres away, behind the glass. It was a peaceful, picturesque scene, and Jacqui acknowledged that she had become attached to the place, both the hospital and the town. But she wouldn't stay on after the nurse she was filling in for came back from long service leave, she suddenly decided. They would have to get someone else to take Greta's place. She would tell Matron on Monday. As she stared out of the window, tears suddenly filled her eyes. Brushing them away, she turned her back on the rapidly approaching dawn. She caught her breath as she confronted David Darling framed in the doorway of her office.

'I—I didn't hear you. . .' she muttered. He was in theatre greens, and looked haggard, as he had that morning after the night of the campaign meeting when he'd been called out. She pushed her black mood aside in her concern. 'Come in and sit down,' she invited at once. 'I'll make you some coffee.'

He came in slowly, hardly taking his eyes off her even to sit down. 'What are you doing here?'

Jacqui busied herself with the coffee-maker, her hands shaking a little. His sudden appearance had completely thrown her. Really, it was ludicrous what this man could do to her composure.

'Jennie's wrenched her ankle. She says it's not too bad, but she thought she ought to rest it. She said she wouldn't be much good if there were a crisis requiring a lot of rushing about, so I told her to rest up and I'd do her shift. She doesn't think she's actually sprained her ankle, so she hopes to be all right by tonight.'

'I suppose Magnusson wasn't too pleased.'

'Kirk? Why would he be concerned about Jennie's ankle?' Jacqui replied evenly.

'Didn't you have a date with him last night?'

'No.'

David's eyes narrowed suspiciously. 'I thought you spent most weekends in his company lately.' He added accusingly, 'Fraternising with the anti-Lakeside lobby.'

'I thought you'd appreciate having a spy in the camp,' she retorted lightly.

He glared. 'Lakeside's nothing to you, and Magnusson can afford to give a woman a good time. He's pretty well-heeled. I'm not surprised you're gadding about with him.'

'Thanks for the insult.' Jacqui refused to let him ride her. 'You're exaggerating, anyway. I've been doing campaign work in most of my free time lately, not gadding about with Kirk. And I do have to wash, iron and do housework. All last night interrupted was my letter-writing.' She looked across the room at his slumped shoulders and felt a great yearning to soothe his tired muscles and ease the tension he was clearly still under. 'Why don't you take your gown off?'

He glanced down and seemed surprised to find he was still wearing it. Half amused, half concerned, Jacqui went to him as he got up again. 'Turn round.' She undid the ties and slipped the green theatre gown off his shoulders, then whipped the cap from his head. 'You look as though you've been up all night too. Emergency op?' She felt a twinge of guilt, remembering her wish earlier in the evening. But she had retracted it, she thought, as consolation.

He raked his hair with long straight fingers. 'Would you believe two?'

'Well, it's been abnormally quiet here, so I guess emergencies had to go somewhere to happen. What were they?'

'First it was an appendicectomy—a very nasty perforation. I'd just finished that and was hoping to go off to bed when a very apologetic young woman and her husband arrived. Their firstborn was about to make his or her appearance. It was soon obvious that there was acute foetal distress and she wasn't going to deliver normally. Immediate Caesarean section was indicated.'

'You have been busy!' Jacqui forced a light tone. 'No wonder you look as though you could do with a rest cure yourself. How are the mother and baby?'

'We were too late. The baby died.'

'Oh, David, I'm sorry. . .' Instinctively she put her arms around him. 'It's awful when that happens.'

'We tried to resuscitate, of course, but she was premature anyway, and all our technology couldn't breathe life back into her.' David clung to Jacqui for a moment, then disengaged himself. A ghost of a grin tugged at his mouth. 'Doctors don't cry!'

'Some do,' she said softly, biting back her own tears for the unknown parents who had lost their first baby. She pushed him firmly back into the chair. 'Sit down. I'll get that coffee—you need it.'

The coffee and biscuits she offered seemed to revive him and when he spoke next his tone was more amenable. 'Someone mentioned you were in last night, so I came down to see if it was true.' He looked hard at her. 'I expected you to be out on the town on a Saturday night.'

Jacqui said lightly, 'You know where to cadge a good cup of coffee!'

'I needed more than that.'

She arched an eyebrow at him.

His lips stretched a little, but it wasn't a real smile. 'Despite that hair you're always wonderfully calm and unruffled. I needed your serenity.'

'Nice compliment, David,' she said quietly. 'I hope I've been some use.'

He sipped the hot drink, regarding her over the rim of his cup, his dark eyes as disconcerting as always. 'Just what the doctor needed!' he murmured, more of his usual nonchalance and humour returning.

But Rina was also what the doctor needed, Jacqui could not help thinking, with a stab of jealousy. Rina satisfied his other even more personal needs more than adequately, apparently. Rina was the person he wanted to live with. No doubt they had been together last night when he was called out. That was something the girl would have to get used to. She would have to learn that her needs would always take second plce to her partner's calling. Jacqui doubted, from her brief acquaintance with Rina Parkinson, that she would be unselfish enough to adapt readily to this scale of priorities. Where was she now? she wondered. Had back to bed meant back to Rina, at the Darling house in Lorrimer Street, or her own place where she had been waiting patiently, or impatiently, for her lover to return?

'The first shift will be arriving soon,' Jacqui said after a silence, and hinting at his departure. 'So will break-fast.' It was causing her more pain than she'd thought possible looking at David and imagining Rina in his arms, Rina caring for him at emotional times like now. Would she be able to provide the comfort he would expect—and need? Why should I care? Jacqui thought. Why am I getting uptight about it?

'And you need the chair!' he said, getting up. 'OK, I can take a hint.' He reached for the gown and cap he'd discarded, and Jacqui said,

'I'll dispose of them. You'd better go and apologise to Rina for ruining her Saturday night.'

His eyes narrowed and his face became tense. 'How did you know I was with Rina when the call came? I didn't tell you.'

'Oh, I'm quite good at putting two and two together, especially when I've been well primed.' She sounded arch even to herself, and was sorry she'd let her own feelings get behind words she shouldn't have said. It was not her business whom he spent his Saturday, or any other nights, with.

'Well primed?' he queried, frowning at her.

Jacqui sought a quick exit from the subject. 'I had coffee with Rina in town yesterday morning, and she told me how it was with you two. It's OK, David. I'm not bothered. Nothing to get steamed up about.'

He had grabbed her by the shoulders and was looking fiercely into her face. 'What the hell are you talking about?' he rasped. 'What did she tell you?'

Jacqui could have bitten her tongue off for the waspish way she had spoken. She had come close to giving herself away with her clumsiness. 'Only that you were on the point of living together but had put it off because of her recent ill health and both your parents' absence. Don't worry, I won't broadcast it.'

David clapped a hand to his forehead and moved away from her. 'Oh, my God!' He turned back. 'I think I'd better explain about Rina.'

'There's no need, David. You don't have any obligation to me just because you—you kissed me a few times. It meant as little to me as it did to you. I was fully aware it wasn't the start of something, and that you never intended it to be, any more than I did.

People sometimes can't avoid striking a few sparks off each other.'

He seemed stunned for a minute, then said, 'And is it just as temporary a thing with Magnusson?'

She managed to shrug, and smile, but the part of her that was hurt couldn't resist giving in to the temptation to prick his ego a little. Why should he be allowed to think that just because she treated him lightly, she treated every man the same? 'That remains to be seen, I suppose,' she said.

The dark blue eyes were withering. 'There's no point, then, in my explaining anything. I guess Magnusson does have quite a lot going for him, even if he is anti-Lakeside, and at least he doesn't get called out in the middle of the night, lucky devil.' His tone was more scathing than envious. He rubbed his unshaven chin and cheeks. 'I'd better be off. Thanks for the coffee.'

In his usual swift, decisive manner, he was gone, leaving Jacqui to pick up his gown and cap and bundle them for the laundry bin. She held the crumpled green garments in her hands for a moment, hugging them against her as though the man were still within. Never before had she hurt so much inside.

CHAPTER NINE

BY THE time Open Day arrived, the campaign to prevent Lakeside being closed down had gathered momentum. There had been public meetings, debates on radio and television and in the local papers, and David in particular had come in for a fair bit of hostility from the councillors and other townspeople who were in favour of the closedown. But he was undeterred.

'We'll win,' he told Jacqui confidently. 'It'll have to come up again at the next council meeting, and I feel pretty certain the plan will be thrown out this time. Marvel Resorts are obviously not so sure of themselves now, because Jack Farringdon told me they've been making tentative overtures to him recently. He's the farmer who owns the alternative site on the other side of the lake. Obviously they'd prefer this site, but it seems they're not necessarily going to go elsewhere if they don't get it. That'll clinch it with some people. Maneroo has distinct tourist possibilities for anyone who gets in first. The only one to lose out will be whoever was aiming to get a nice commission for twisting the council's arm over the preferred position at a preferred price.'

'Was anyone actually doing that?' Jacqui was shocked.

He gave her an unreadable look. 'I'm not prepared to libel anyone, but I have a pretty fair idea. Marvel Resorts were no doubt willing to pay quite handsomely for someone local influential enough to lobby for favoured treatment.' He smiled at her naïveté. 'It's not unusual in deals like this for all sorts of people to get kickbacks, not necessarily in cash, but in business concessions. It's not illegal. One or two business people in this town would probably benefit more than others.'

Jacqui supposed he knew what he was talking about. She hoped, in the circumstances, that David's confidence would be justified. She said, 'We're all set for tomorrow. Staff are primed to present the hospital in its very best light, to emphasise the importance of it to Maneroo, and to collect signatures. I guarantee there won't be a single visitor who'll get away without buying a badge, car sticker and signing a petition.'

'Great. You've done a grand job organising it all, Jacqui. Any T-shirts left?'

'We'll all be wearing them, and quite a lot have sold already. I ordered some more, and they arrived yesterday, thank goodness. I got more children's sizes this time.' She chuckled. 'Kids make good propaganda!'

Open Day began about ten in the morning, and by eleven the hospital and grounds were seething with visitors eager to see their community hospital at work. People were encouraged to visit the wards and treatment-rooms, the A and E department, and the various facilities. The maternity wards were as usual among the most popular.

Everywhere they went visitors were confronted by posters extolling the virtues of the hospital, the importance of it to the community, and were reminded of what the loss of it would mean.

Stalls at suitable points were selling the badges, T-shirts and car stickers that Jacqui had organised and collecting the signatures on petition forms. There was

some lively discussion with people who insisted that
Hindmarsh could better supply the medical needs of
the community and that Maneroo needed a centrally
situated tourist complex more than the hospital. David
had briefed all the staff thoroughly on the arguments
in favour of keeping the hospital, so no one was caught
without convincing responses. Not all members of the
hospital board of management were in favour of keeping Lakeside open, but those who were, fortunately
the majority, turned out to lend their support.

'If there were any waverers,' Jacqui said at the end
of the day, 'I reckon they'd have to be won over now.'
She showered petition forms across her desk. 'When
these are plonked down on the table at the council
meeting, I reckon they'll have to take notice.' She was
flushed with success and more optimistic than she had
ever been.

David had joined her in her office after the last
visitors had left. He looked pleased too. They had
worked well together, Jacqui thought. He had been
more distant with her at the personal level recently, for
which she should have been grateful, but instead, every
time she saw him, she still wanted to throw herself
headlong into his arms. She could hardly wait now for
her time at Lakeside to end. There were only another
couple of weeks to go before Marion Martin returned.
Jacqui hadn't yet decided what she was going to do
then.

'It was a highly successful Open Day,' David said.
'Best we've ever had.' He grasped her arms. 'Thanks
for everything, Jacqui. You did a grand job.'

'I had a lot of willing and able helpers. Everyone did
their bit. In fact, I'm not sure that the denizens of
Maneroo don't know a little *too* much about how their

community hospital works. We didn't half blow our own trumpets!'

David's arms fell to his sides and he stepped back as though regretting the impulsive intimacy. 'More *glasnost* in the medical arena is no bad thing. At least they should now have a better idea of how we spend the profit we make on the tombola at the annual fête!'

'What was amazing,' said Jacqui, 'was that we had no emergencies either in the hospital or arriving at A and E.'

A glint of humour appeared in his eyes. 'Wouldn't you have liked to demonstrate our speed and efficiency in a crisis?'

She shook her head. 'We couldn't have let the public see that kind of action and I'm sure you were glad not to be called away. It was important you were around to answer questions and put your case in person to individuals.'

David looked at her steadily for a moment. 'I suppose you wouldn't be free to have dinner with me tonight?'

Jacqui was so surprised that, rather rashly, she spoke her immediate thought. 'Does that mean you've had a tiff with Rina again?' She sounded arch without intending to. She ought to have stopped herself making such a blunt remark.

His reaction was immediate and strong. 'You've got entirely the wrong idea about Rina.'

'Have I? I thought it was well known that you and she had an on-again, off-again relationship.'

'That's her version. The relationship is one-sided. Always has been.'

Jacqui raised a sceptical eyebrow. 'But she told me

that as soon as your parents return you'll be setting up house with her.'

He clutched his hair in anguish. 'She has a very vivid imagination.'

'Or you've been leading her on. . .'

Anger now flashed into the dark blue eyes. 'God, Jacqui, what sort of man do you think I am? She's a kid. . .scarcely more than eighteen!'

'That makes her an adult. Most men prefer younger women.'

David swivelled to face her squarely. 'Look, you'd better get this straight. I am not romantically involved with Rina. Her parents are very good friends of my parents. She's had an adolescent crush on me for longer than is good for her. I thought she'd grow out of it, but she's still very immature and, despite everything I've said, now seems to have deceived herself into believing I'll eventually marry her or live with her or whatever it is her vivid imagination proposes.'

Jacqui was stunned by this revelation, and his vehemence, but not wholly convinced. 'You see a lot of her,' she said, wondering why she didn't just tell him she had things to do, and cease torturing herself with this sort of conversation.

'I try not to,' he answered with so much feeling she almost believed him. 'But it's difficult. . .she makes constant demands. . .' His eyes met Jacqui's. 'She's as much a medical problem as a personal one. You've probably noticed that she's anorexic.'

'I thought it highly likely.'

He shocked her further. 'A while ago she threatened to starve herself to death if I didn't take her seriously.'

Jacqui was appalled. 'Do you mean that?'

'Unfortunately, yes. And so did she. I managed to

persuade her that I'd never take anyone seriously who behaved as stupidly as she was doing. It worked, temporarily, and she agreed to go down to Melbourne to stay with a friend for a few weeks, promising to try and put on weight.' He paused, then said ruefully, 'The night you arrived and I was so rude to you, I'd just come from a highly emotional confrontation with Rina. I hoped for a change in attitude after that breakaway, but all that's happened is that she's twisted my ultimatum into a virtual promise. I'm having a hell of a time with her all over again at the moment. What makes it worse is that I'm supposed to be keeping an eye on her while her parents are away. She's doing all she can to take advantage of that!' He looked really anxious. 'I have to go gently with her, because I'm afraid of what she'll do, but I can't marry the girl!'

Jacqui said drily, 'Rina said neither of you believes in marriage. But she seemed very sure you were practically "engaged". Her way of describing living together?'

He tightened his mouth and was silent for a moment. When he spoke at last, there was unexpected emotion in his voice. 'I do believe in marriage, Jacqui. But only with the right person.'

'Maybe living with Rina will show you that she is the right one,' Jacqui said, wishing they could get off the topic.

'I have no intention of living with Rina, or anyone!'

'Look, David, it's nothing to do with me whether you live with Rina or marry her or neither,' said Jacqui. 'It's none of my business. I shouldn't have mentioned it.'

'I wonder why you did.'

Her cheeks warmed and she had no ready answer.

She turned away and pretended to look at some case notes in front of her. She wished he would go.

He did not move, but seemed to be weighing up what he was going to say next. At last he took a deep breath and said, 'I'm going to tell you something not even Rina knows. When I was in the UK, just after I qualified, I fell in love with a girl and we got engaged.'

He paused, and Jacqui stifled her gasp of surprise. She looked up at him. 'But not married?'

'No. It was a crazy spur-of-the-moment thing, and it didn't last.' He laughed harshly. 'I was naïvely romantic then. I came down to earth with a horrible jolt when I realised she'd been two-timing me, almost from the day we were engaged. She made a fool of me. She eventually dumped me for a charismatic sports hero, who was evidently more romantic, and much more well-heeled, than a newly qualified doctor. Fortunately only my parents and a few close friends knew about Elise.' His mouth quirked slightly while his gaze lingered on her face, forcing her to look away. 'Since then I've been very wary of committing myself, very distrustful. It's not that I don't believe in marriage, but you don't beat yourself twice with the same stick. Whenever I'm tempted, the memory of Elise mocks me. No man likes being made a fool of.'

No woman does either, Jacqui thought, and was almost tempted to tell him about Carey. But sympathising with each other would get them nowhere. Without looking at him, she said, 'I dare say Rina wouldn't make a fool of you?'

'That isn't the point. I'm not in love with Rina.'

If what he had said was true, and Jacqui still wasn't sure she believed him, it did seem that Rina had been making up her story for Jacqui's benefit, and perhaps even to delude herself. David was staring morosely out of the window when Jacqui dared to look at him again. She felt a strange mix of sympathy and exasperation with him. One day perhaps he might fall in love again so deeply, he'd take a chance on it lasting, but obviously he didn't feel that way about her. Even more obvious to her now was what she had been afraid to admit before, that she was deeply and irrevocably in love with David.

'So what do I do, Sister Brent?' he asked, turning. A faintly mocking smile hovered on his lips which she suddenly ached to kiss. 'How do I get myself out of this mess?'

Using deliberate lightness as a control on her feelings, Jacqui said, 'I'd say flee overseas, but you're too embroiled in hospital affairs at the moment to do that, I suppose.'

He struck his forehead with a spread palm. 'Oh, God, yes.'

'It's tricky, then. I really don't know what you can do. You're in a spot, David.'

'Which I'm sure you think serves me right,' he said. 'You think it's my own fault for leading the girl on, but I swear I never have——'

'It's not my place to pass judgement,' Jacqui said, speaking with difficulty because her own feelings were becoming deeply involved. She managed a smile, however. 'I suppose you can't help being the kind of man to turn a young impressionable girl's head.'

'What?'

'Oh, come on, don't be modest. You're a charmer and you know it. You *exercise* your charm. It's not your fault if it has dire results. Not everyone is sensible and mature enough not to take you seriously.'

'Like you,' he murmured rather drily.

If only you knew, thought Jacqui, flinching. She said, 'Young girls fall in and out of love quite often as a rule. It may simply require time to solve your problem. Maybe Rina will come to her senses soon.'

'A lot of help you are! You think it's just a joke.' He laughed, but the despairing tone was still there in his voice. He added with some feeling, 'Well, at least Magnusson isn't likely to threaten to starve himself to death if you refuse to marry him or live with him.' He looked at her stonily. 'I suppose he accepts the fact that you're here today but gone tomorrow.'

Jacqui said nothing. She didn't want to discuss Kirk with him, since David clearly disliked the other man. 'I'd better get on,' she said after the silence had become awkward. 'I've got quite a lot to do before I leave.'

He heaved himself off the edge of her desk. 'So have I.' He looked so dejected as he lunged for the door that Jacqui said,

'David. . .'

He turned abruptly. 'Yes?'

'I'm not laughing at you. I'm sorry your early experience with falling in love was so painful. And I do believe you have a real problem with Rina and that she's psychologically unstable. I'm sure you agree she needs psychiatric treatment.'

He leaned on the still closed door and clasped his head in both hands, looking at her with his deep anxiety fully revealed in his face. 'Yes. But you can't order an eighteen-year-old girl to go to a psychiatrist and talk over her problems when she doesn't believe she has any. As you pointed out, she's an adult and can make her own decisions. The trouble is, she's behaving like a child.'

'Maybe when her parents return, you could talk to them.'

He shook his head. 'They'd be no help. Rina doesn't get on with them—never has. She lives at home, but it's a tense, rather abrasive relationship. She always felt left out, I think, when her twin brothers came along. She felt her parents favoured them more than her.'

'A classic case of insecurity.'

'Yes. I suppose that's why she turned to me.'

'Father figure?'

He pulled a face. 'I *am* old enough to be her father! Just!'

'What do the Parkinsons think of their daughter's obsession? Do they know?'

'They'd be delighted with whoever took Rina off their hands. She's been a problem all her life.'

Jacqui said thoughtfully, 'What she needs is friends of her own age.'

'So I've told her,' he said resignedly. 'She says they bore her.'

'Have you told her young people bore you?'

'That's the trouble, Jacqui. I'm scared to be too direct with her. She just bursts into tears, says she's got nobody but me, and if I don't care about her she might as well kill herself.'

'Emotional blackmail is difficult to fight.'

'It can wear you down,' he said disconsolately. 'I can see myself giving in.'

Was that what he really wanted to do? And was he just afraid, because Rina was so young, that she would eventually make a fool of him as Elise had? Jacqui said tersely, 'Rina's a very attractive girl. She could be beautiful.'

His face darkened angrily. 'Are you suggesting that would be compensation?'

'You're fond of her too, aren't you?'

'I was. I thought of myself as a sort of Dutch uncle when she was growing up. I never dreamed she'd become obsessed with me. I don't really have any feeling for her now except pity. She's just a selfish, clinging, emotional millstone, but I can't be cruel to her, Jacqui.'

Jacqui smiled. 'No, you would never be that, but perhaps you have to be cruel to be kind in this case. Maybe you should take a chance and be really tough with her. Call her bluff. I'm sorry, David, I know that doesn't help.'

He said impulsively, 'Do me a favour, Jacqui? Break your date with Magnusson and have dinner with me tonight. Take my mind off this dreadful impasse.'

Jacqui desperately wanted to say yes, but she dared not. She was too afraid that she might prove too willing to let him find solace in her arms. Like poor Rina, she was obsessed with the man, and she had even less chance than Rina of finding happiness with him.

'I'm sorry, I can't do that,' she said, even though it wasn't true.

His mouth thinned and he shoved his hands deep into his coat pockets. 'No, I suppose you couldn't. Presumptuous of me to ask.'

He flung the door open and vanished through it with characteristic speed. Jacqui choked back tears and hoped no one would come in until she had composed herself.

That Saturday evening promised to be one of the dreariest of Jacqui's life. She prepared a solitary meal and ate it in front of the television, trying desperately to distract her mind from thoughts of David Darling. His confessions about Rina and his failed relationship with Elise had moved her deeply and she was still trying to think of some way to help him. She couldn't bear to see him in such an impossible situation. He didn't deserve that. She swayed between anger and pity for Rina Parkinson, and fear that David might marry the girl because he could see no other solution gnawed at her.

Finally she decided to go out. The big screen at the cinema might prove a better distraction than TV. She had just switched off the television when the telephone rang, and she answered it reluctantly, in no mood to gossip with anyone. It was Li.

'Did you realise you left your handbag here?' the Vietnamese girl asked.

Jacqui was startled. 'I did?' She glanced at the chair where she usually tossed it on arriving home. There was a supermarket carrier bag sitting there, forgotten.

'I found it on the floor between the desk and the wall,' said Li. 'Only a moment ago.'

Jacqui clapped a hand to her forehead. 'I remember now. I was just leaving and the phone rang. It was the tomatoes. . .'

'Tomatoes?' Li sounded puzzled and amused.

'Mrs Wakefield's husband brought me some tomatoes today, in a carrier bag. I put my keys in my pocket and shoved my bag in the carrier, then I dumped it on the desk when I answered the phone. I didn't notice that my bag had fallen out. I must be going dotty, Li. I flung the carrier on a chair and I haven't looked at it since. I forgot all about the tomatoes. Isn't that stupid?'

Li laughed. 'Sometimes we do silly things when we

are preoccupied. What shall I do? Lock the bag in the filing cabinet?'

'No, I'll come over and get it,' said Jacqui. 'I'm going out anyway, and I'll need it.' When Jacqui arrived at Lakeside, she found the staff in a bit of a stir.

'It's Ruby Wentworth,' Li told her. 'She's gone missing.'

'She's one of the Alzheimer's in Geriatric, isn't she?' Jacqui had visited in the geriatric ward a few times on days off. Ruby was a long-time patient.

'Yes. She's always wandering off somewhere, but usually someone spots her before she even gets out of the building. I don't know exactly what happened this time, except that they've been searching for half an hour and can't find her.'

'She's probably still in the building,' Jacqui said. 'It's nearly dark. She wouldn't go out in the dark.'

Li wasn't so sure. 'Janice, who's worked on Geriatric for ages, says they'll do anything. Alzheimer's can be very unpredictable.'

Jacqui went along to the geriatric ward to see if she could help the search, but Janice assured her that there were already plenty of people looking and that they would be alerting the police if they didn't find the old lady in the next half-hour.

'Just in case she's taken it into her head to toddle into town in her nightdress,' said Janice. 'One of my old darlings did that once and went to the pictures, normal as anything, and no one even noticed she had a nightgown under her cardi. But the lucid period didn't last. Afterwards she was so confused she didn't know where she was.'

'I'm on my way to the cinema,' Jacqui said. 'I'll keep a look out!'

'She'll turn up,' said Janice. 'She can't come to much harm even if she has strayed out into the grounds. I'm sure they'll find her soon.'

'I hope so.' Jacqui went back to her car. It was nearly dark now. She had already missed the start of the programme, but she would still be in time for the main feature. She drove, however, at the stipulated slow speed along the driveway, and it was just as she was approaching the entrance that a flash of something white a short distance away between two large island shrubberies caught her eye. Could it have been an old lady in a nightdress?

She stopped the car and got out. She walked quickly through the avenue of poplars that lined the driveway, peering into the gloom, but could see nothing.

'Mrs Wentworth!' she called. 'Ruby! Is that you, Ruby?'

The sudden reappearance of the white-clad figure around the edge of the island shrubbery just ahead startled her. It was close enough to be identified as an old woman. She had a walking-stick in her hand, but in spite of it, as she tried to run, she was stumbling and almost falling over. Jacqui set off after her. She did not rush as she didn't want to frighten the old lady any more than she had already. It wasn't going to be hard to catch up with her, but it might be rather more difficult to persuade her to go back to the hospital.

Eventually Ruby stopped and looked around, confused and alarmed. Jacqui stepped quietly up to her side and pulled the old woman's free arm through hers, gripping the gnarled hand firmly.

'Hello, Ruby,' she said. 'What a lovely evening for a

walk. But it's getting a little cool, don't you think? Shall we go back now?' Gently she began to propel the old lady back towards the driveway. Ruby offered no resistance, but muttered and mumbled incoherently. Jacqui talked to her in soothing tones and patted her arm comfortingly.

They were skirting one of the island shrubberies when a dark figure loomed up out of the shadows and the beam of a torch dazzled them.

'I found her back there a way,' Jacqui said, shading her eyes from the glare. She assumed it was someone from the hospital searching the grounds. 'She's OK. Who's that?'

The torch went out, but no one spoke. The darkness by contrast seemed suddenly deeper. Jacqui had time for only a second of puzzlement and fear before a hand was clapped roughly over her mouth, she was wrenched away from the old lady, and a rasping voice in her ear said, 'Scream and I'll strangle you.' Her attacker's other hand wrenched her arm painfully behind her back.

Last time might have been imagination, Jacqui thought as chill fear ran through her, but this time her attacker was real, horrifyingly and sickeningly real. A faint smell of disinfectant, the familiar 'hospital' brand, drifted from him and she realised with a shock that he must be from the hospital. He probably was in the search party for the old lady, but coming on her like this he had snatched at an opportunity.

As he dragged her away towards the shrubbery, she struggled wildly, despite his threat, trying to kick back at him, flailing her free arm, but he threatened her again and twisted her arm until it burned. He was taller than her, and very strong. One of the technicians? she thought, her mind wildly picturing them one by one. One of the two male nurses? She couldn't be sure. She was only sure it was someone from the hospital. He was not wearing a mask, and would know that she would discover eventually who he was. . .which meant that he wouldn't want her to get away. . .alive.

Oh, no, she thought in panic, he'll kill me! She made a valiant effort to escape, but he was too strong and threw her to the ground. Jacqui fell heavily on her side, which almost stunned her, but she lifted her arm to ward off the impending descent of the shadowy form looming over her and averted her face. This couldn't be happening, it couldn't. . .

Discovering that she could open her mouth again was useless, as fear and her hard impact with the ground had robbed her of breath. To her amazement, however, she heard someone screaming, and the sound wasn't coming from her. It was more a kind of wailing than screaming, and it seemed to blot out everything. She heard her assailant curse, 'Bloody hell!' and then it seemed as if all hell was let loose.

Looking up, she saw the strangest sight of her life; an old woman in a nightdress beating the man with a walking-stick and screaming at him. It was too dark to see much more than the whiteness of the nightdress, but by the old lady's stance Jacqui realised her assailant had tripped and fallen over. He would be up again in a minute, though, and no doubt would be incensed enough to kill them both. As Jacqui scrambled to her feet, instinctively going to the assistance of the old lady, however futile that might prove to be in this deserted part of the grounds, two people came running on to the scene flashing torches.

Somebody pulled the ferocious old lady away from the figure on the ground.

'Heavens, what got into her? She's half killed him! Ronnie, for God's sake what's going on?' They were helping her attacker up. They didn't realise. . .

Summoning all her breath, Jacqui shouted, 'Don't let him get away! He attacked me. . .' She recognised him now. He was one of the technicians, one who assisted the movement of patients to and from the operating theatre, who came only rarely into Medical but who always looked at her and other nurses long and hard. 'He gives me the creeps,' Pauline, the rather nervous nursing aide, had said once. But Jacqui had never been suspicious, and neither had anyone else, apparently.

Her presence startled the newcomers so much that their attention was momentarily distracted. The man, Ronnie, took advantage of it and made a dash into the darkness. One of the others sped after him, but Jacqui guessed he'd never catch him.

'Ronnie?' said the other, an older man, John Carstairs. 'I can't believe it! You say he attacked you?'

Jacqui nodded and whispered, 'Yes. I think he may be the prowler we've been troubled by every so often.' The beam of the torch showed her the old lady now squatting hunched and silent, stuffing the bunched-up cloth of her nightgown into her mouth. Jacqui went to her and put her arms around her and held her close. 'You saved me life, Ruby,' she said in a hoarse whisper.

Surprisingly, Ruby spoke. She said quite distinctly, 'They'll never get *my* money, the devils!'

Tears poured down Jacqui's face as she stroked the old woman's hair. 'It's all right, Ruby,' she whispered, 'we're safe now, and so's your money.'

Suddenly another voice stabbed the darkness. 'What's going on? What was all that noise? Good God, Jacqui, what are you doing here?'

Jacqui felt liquid with relief. It was David. She couldn't see his face behind the beam of his torch. But in any case tears were still streaming down her face, blurring her vision.

John Carstairs summed up the situation for him. 'Sister's pretty shocked, I reckon, David,' he said in a low voice. 'It seems she found Ruby, then Ronnie found them both, and attacked Sister Brent. Fortunately, for reasons of her own, Ruby set about him with her walking-stick, screaming like a banshee. Tom Glass and I heard the racket and ran to see what was up. We pulled the old lady off him and were getting Ronnie up when Sister yelled that he'd attacked her. She reckons he's the prowler we've been bothered with. I thought she'd gone mad until Ronnie suddenly lit off. I guess that proves it. Tom went after him.'

David came to Jacqui and gathered both her and the old lady tightly against him. 'You lunatic! Looking for her in the dark by yourself. Are you mad?'

'I caught a glimpse of her from the driveway and chased after her,' Jacqui explained. She buried her head against David's chest. 'Oh, David, it was so horrible! I thought he was going to rape me, and then he'd kill me because I'd know he was from the hospital.'

David said quietly, 'You'd better stick around in case Tom comes back, John. I think I'd better get these two back to the hospital—they're both shivering.'

David helped the two women the rest of the way back to the driveway and into Jacqui's car. He turned it round and drove back to the hospital. In no time at all, Ruby Wentworth was in bed, while Jacqui was recovering with hot tea and a brandy in David's sitting-room and refusing absolutely to be put to bed like a patient.

'I'm all right,' she insisted. 'He didn't hurt me. Well, I may have a couple of bruises, but I'm OK, really I am, David.' In fact she felt extraordinarily calm now, and that was because he was with her, she thought. How she'd feel when she got home, she wasn't sure, but it had to be faced. She wasn't going to be fussed over.

'You should stay the night here,' David advised.

'No way,' she insisted. 'I'm going home.'

They argued for a bit and she won. David agreed so long as she let him drive her home. It was only ten o'clock but seemed much later. So much had happened in the last couple of hours. Tom and John had returned, but Ronnie had got away from them. The police had been alerted and were looking out for him. Jacqui hoped fervently that they would catch him. If not he would leave town and maybe turn up somewhere else, under another name, and harass or maybe even harm others.

David came into the flat with her and checked her security. Then he looked long and hard at her and said decisively, 'I'm not leaving you alone tonight. Don't argue. That guy knows who you are, where you live, and that you know him. This is much worse than last time. You've had a hell of an experience and you're suffering from shock. I'm staying, Jacqui. I want to be sure you're safe.'

Jacqui bit her lip. She could see it would be no use arguing. 'I'll fetch some blankets and make you up a bed on the couch,' she said.

David said, 'Thanks.'

CHAPTER TEN

WHEN Jacqui woke next morning the sun was just up, casting a shimmering beam across her bed. She listened tensely, aware that some unusual sound had awoken her. Someone was moving about in her kitchen. She stiffened with apprehension as the horror of the previous night swept over her, and a sudden surge of fear made swallowing difficult. But as she came fully awake she remembered with a flood of relief that David had stayed the night. To protect her.

She slid out of bed and threw on her cotton dressing-gown. Barefoot, she padded along to the kitchen to see what he was doing. The rich aroma of freshly made coffee drifted to her before she even opened the door.

'Good morning!'

David turned from the window bench where he was supervising the toaster. 'Good morning, Jacqui!' He was unshaven and dishevelled, his tawny hair spiking up all over his head, but Jacqui thought he had never looked more handsome or desirable. Her breath caught in her throat, making further words impossible for a minute.

David said, 'Did I wake you? I tried to be very quiet. I was going to bring you some breakfast shortly.'

She smiled. 'Really? Breakfast in bed? Goodness, I can't remember when I last enjoyed that luxury.'

'Go back to bed and enjoy it this morning.' He jammed two more slices of bread in the toaster and left it, coming across the room to her. He took her hands in his. 'Are you all right?'

'Yes I'm fine.' Her mouth and nose felt a little tender, and her arm was aching from being twisted so cruelly, but there appeared to be no actual bruising.

'You managed to sleep?'

'Yes, I did.' She sidled away from him, emotionally disturbed by his nearness. 'I'm pretty tough, David. Nurses are!'

She wasn't all that tough, David thought. She was as vulnerable as any woman. White-hot anger flamed in him as he grappled with the knowledge of what would have happened to her if Ruby Wentworth hadn't beaten off her attacker and John and Tom hadn't arrived in time. He hadn't quite come to terms with it yet, but he knew one thing—last night had been a watershed in his life.

He raised a smile. 'Not as tough as old Ruby!'

Jacqui shook her head in wonderment. 'She was fantastic. I'm not sure she was laying into him for the right reasons, but I'm thankful she did. She said afterwards, "They'll never get *my* money, the devils." I think she must have thought we were being mugged.'

'Just as well she took her walking stick with her.'

'Yes, it was lucky for me she did, although I suspect she'd have taken to him with her bare hands anyway. I think it was her terrible screaming that threw him off guard completely. It was eerie, David.' She shuddered. 'I hope she's all right.'

'I'm sure she will be. In fact by today she'll have forgotten it all, I expect. She won't even remember wandering out of the hospital.' He paused, looking deeply into her eyes. 'You were both very brave.'

Jacqui looked away and said, 'Are you going to offer me any of that delicious-smelling coffee?'

'I hope you don't mind my invading your kitchen.'

'Not if I'm to be waited on.'

They ate breakfast without saying much. The events of the previous night had had a sobering effect which both were feeling, as well as reaction to the shock. Finally, Jacqui said, 'Thanks for staying last night, David. I really appreciate it.'

'I couldn't have let you sleep here alone.' He looked at the clock on the wall. 'Let's hear the news. They might have caught our Ronnie by now.'

Jacqui switched on the radio. It was not quite time for the news bulletin. She poured more coffee and was about to raise the cup to her lips when the phone rang. She ran to answer it, and was back in a very short time.

'That was the police,' she said. 'They got him. They've told the hospital already.' Relief made her feel weak, as though her muscles had melted away. She sank back into her chair and buried her face in her hands.

'Thank God,' said David. 'Now maybe we can relax. I dare say he's been responsible for all the reports of prowlers in the town. It'll be a great relief to everyone.'

'To think he worked at the hospital all the time,' Jacqui mused. 'I always felt uneasy with him, it was the way he looked at you, but I never dreamt——'

'Don't think about it.' David reached across the table and covered her hand with his.

She couldn't tell him that she wasn't now, that she was thinking more about him, relishing his presence in her kitchen, savouring this Sunday morning intimacy because all too soon he would get up and go home and she would be alone again.

'I'd better be going,' he said after a moment. 'I'll sneak out quietly, so your reputation won't be tarnished.'

Jacqui carried the breakfast dishes to the sink. She didn't want him to go, but there was no point in trying to delay him. He was only there because he had been protective of her, and now that Ronnie was in custody she had no more need of him.

She said, 'The others in the house sleep in on Sundays if they've been out late, and they all would have been last night. No one will see you.'

David rose and was standing very close to her as she turned from the sink. With her bright copper hair tumbling in disarray over her shoulders, framing her pale beautiful face, she caused an almost unbearable ache in him. He could not prevent his hands moving to rest on her shoulders, or his head moving so that his lips touched hers. The contact was electric. He wrapped his arms around her slender form and kissed her deeply and emotionally, releasing some of the tension that had been building in him ever since he had been forced to confront his personal feelings about the danger she had been in last night.

Jacqui discovered that she was too weak to resist him. She wanted David's arms around her more than anything else in the world, and his lips on hers. His care and protection last night had deepened her feelings for him even more, although she knew he would have done the same for anyone. What she had feared was happening; she would not be able to deny him the full expression of her love. That it was not reciprocated no longer mattered.

His warm hands cupped her face, thumbs gently

caressing her cheeks, his eyes full of longing. 'Jacqui, you torment me so. . .'

His mouth made another crushing assault on hers, but there was no pain, only exquisite pleasure in his skilful arousal of her senses. When he curved a hand gently over her breast, teasing the hardening nipple beneath the thin covering of her nightdress, and then slipped the shoulder down to bear its nakedness for his mouth, Jacqui was lost. For a moment the fires kindled by his sensual touch raged within her, and she tangled desperate fingers in his hair. When he scooped her up and carried her into her bedroom, she was as eager as a bride for fulfilment. He slipped off her dressing-gown and nightdress, and discarded his own clothes as quickly.

'Jacqui, Jacqui. . .my sweet one, my beautiful darling. . .' he was whispering with a breathless huskiness between fiery kisses as he lay beside her.

I love you, she said, but she said it silently, because she knew he would not want to hear it. His endearments were not to be taken seriously. She knew she was a fool, but she didn't care. She loved him. She loved the sound of his voice and the scent of his body. She loved the gentleness of his hands and even the raspiness of his unshaven cheeks and chin on her own soft skin. She exulted in his muscular strength and infinite tenderness. She loved the sweet, sensual things he was whispering to her. For a brief time he was hers and hers alone. It would have to be enough.

'You're wonderful,' he told her in the soft, dreamy aftermath of lovemaking.

She snuggled against his side, reluctant to admit reality yet. 'You're OK yourself.'

'Is that a typical British understatement, or an exaggeration?'

'It's intended to keep your ego in check.'

But he didn't say 'I love you' and she didn't expect him to. She let him use her shower and gave him a throwaway razor to scrape his chin. She made him lunch, but she didn't allow herself to think further than the present moment which was hers to relish. At some point she might have to decide whether to let the affair continue until she left, or to nip it in the bud right away, but decisions were not a necessary part of that languid Sunday.

Before he left her, David suddenly said as though it were an instant decision, 'I may have to go to Melbourne tomorrow for a couple of days. There are few urgent personal matters I need to attend to.'

Jacqui felt the pang of loss at once. She said lightly, 'How will we manage without you?'

'The VMOs will cope.' He held her face in his hands and kissed her lips. 'Will my tempestuous redhead miss me?'

'She might!'

He gripped her shoulders tightly, gaze darkening. 'I don't want anyone else poaching on my preserves. You can tell Magnusson you're busy.'

'That's a bit high-handed.'

'Jacqui. . .' he pleaded '. . .don't torment me.' He let her hair sweep through his fingers. 'God, you're beautiful. I don't know what I would have done if anything had happened to you last night. . .' He lowered his lips to within a hair's breadth of hers. His last kiss was brief and hard, and, as usual, he made an abrupt exit.

* * *

Loving David made Jacqui nurture what she knew was a futile hope, but she couldn't help it, even though she kept telling herself that for David making love to her had been pleasant but unimportant. He would never make the kind of commitment to her that she knew she must have from a man if she was to be happy.

David stayed away for several days, and life in the hospital went on as before, with quiet times and crises. The only difference was that, instead of David, visiting medical officers, two local GPs, Dr Prentiss and Dr Forster were on call for all emergencies, not just their own patients' needs.

Jacqui missed David's daily visit to her ward more than she would have thought possible. For a day or two the arrest of Ronnie and the end of the prowler affair was the hot topic of conversation, but that soon diminished. Jacqui went several times to see Mrs Wentworth, but the old lady seemed to have no recollection of any untoward experience—which, Jacqui thought, was probably just as well.

For some reason, on Wednesday morning, Jacqui suddenly thought about Carey for the first time in a long while. His case had been adjourned and she had lost track of it. She had not had time recently, with all the campaign activities, to read the newspaper thoroughly, and the electronic media had found more interesting and salacious news to report.

The thought was fleeting, but she must have been psychic, she thought, when she picked up a newspaper in the nurses' room where she was having her sandwiches because there had been thundery showers all morning, and saw a report on the case. The trial had been short, over three days, in the end, and Carey had been sentenced to two years in gaol. There was a picture of him, handsome, smiling, debonair, taken obviously in the good times. But he would survive, she thought. He would live to charm a few more women and deceive a few more gullible people. She wondered how she could ever have likened David to him. David had the same kind of charm in a way, but underneath he was a totally different person. She almost wished he weren't; it would be easier to live without him.

Lissa rang that night. 'Did you see the piece in the paper about Carey?' she asked.

'Yes, I did. I couldn't feel too sorry for him,' Jacqui admitted.

'I should hope not!' Lissa went on, 'Jacqui. . . I've been thinking. I don't know whether it's because you've been gone, but I've been feeling homesick lately. I think I'll go home for Christmas.'

'For good?'

'I don't know. I feel restless.' She went on, 'What about you? Do you feel like coming too?'

Jacqui wasn't sure, but the idea had appeal. Especially now. If she didn't want to stay in the UK, she could always come back again, maybe to another state. 'It's a tempting thought,' she said. 'My folks would like it as much as yours, I know.'

'If we give ourselves time,' Lissa said enthusiastically, assuming already that Jacqui would go with her, 'we could take a trip to Sydney or maybe Adelaide and Perth, on the way, and see how we like it in case we decide to come back. I've saved up quite a bit. Could you afford it?'

That idea had appeal too. Taking a look at another state capital city might be a good plan. Perth was said to be picturesque and had a free and easy lifestyle. 'Let me think about it,' Jacqui said. 'I promise I'll let you know quickly.'

She had already decided to leave when Marion returned, so unless she wanted a one-sided temporary affair with David—if that was what he intended—that would inevitably leave her heartbroken and emotionally scarred, she ought not to change her mind about that. She didn't have to think it over for long. It was better to leave sooner rather than later. She decided to ring Lissa at the weekend and tell her she wanted to go along with the plan. At least that was a positive answer to the dilemma of being in love with a man whose own feelings about her were purely physical and who, if he ever did marry, might only do so out of a misguided sense of obligation, a victim of emotional blackmail. Going off with Lissa wouldn't cure her heartache, but it would be better than casting herself out into a lonely limbo.

On Thursday night there was a tennis club dance. At first Jacqui had told Kirk she wouldn't be going, but she felt so depressed at the end of the day, she decided to go after all. There had been no word from David and so far as she knew he wasn't back yet. She was missing him all right, she thought gloomily, as she pulled on a green silk dress that flattered her curves and lent vibrancy to her already vibrant hair. She was always going to miss him. There would never be another man with David's qualities, and David's devastating attractiveness—his special charisma—of that she was certain.

Kirk Magnusson was surprised to see her. His eyes roved admiringly over her. 'You look very ravishing tonight, Jacqui.' He took her hand and stroked it idly. 'I thought you weren't going to come.'

'I changed my mind. I thought I might be too tired, but I feel OK.'

'Dancing helps one to unwind,' he said. 'Shall we make a start?'

Jacqui did not feel comfortable held in his arms. She wished she hadn't come now. Kirk was pleasant, charming, likeable, but no substitute for David. If she couldn't have David in her arms, she would rather not have anyone. But it wasn't so easy to leave now she had arrived. Kirk was with a group of friends and he introduced her, bought her a drink and then danced again and again with her.

It was a hot night and the air-conditioning in the hall was not as efficient as it might have been. People began to open windows and someone drew back the big double doors that led to the patio outside.

'Let's get a drink and go outside,' Kirk suggested. 'It's stifling in here.'

As plenty of other people had the same idea, Jacqui did not demur. Kirk fetched long cold drinks and they escaped into the cooler night air.

'Mmm, that is better,' Jacqui said with relief. 'I was beginning to get a headache.'

They sat at a table for a few minutes with their drinks, and chatted in a desultory fashion.

'Looks as though the pro-Lakeside campaign will win,' Kirk remarked.

'I certainly hope so!'

He smiled. 'I don't hold it against you. I hope you don't hold my views against me?'

'Of course not,' said Jacqui, but in reality she found that she did. She felt restless and edgy and longed to go, but felt she should stick it out for another hour or so. People came and went around them, and some even danced on the patio. Kirk evidently thought that was a good idea and invited Jacqui to do so.

His cheek brushed her hair and he pressed his lips against her temple, his hand around her waist drawing her against him hard. Jacqui was glad when the music from inside the hall stopped and the supper announcement carried out to them.

People immediately headed for the entrance, but Kirk said, 'No rush. There's always plenty for everyone. I hate unseemly crushes for food.'

Jacqui had to agree with that. They lingered, leaning against the patio balustrade, while everyone else went in, and when they were the only ones left Kirk said, smiling, 'Alone at last! You're looking so marvellous tonight, Jacqui, I can't resist you.' He jerked her into his arms and kissed her.

Jacqui was startled. 'Kirk. . .' was all she managed to get out before he was plundering her mouth again with a ferocity that repelled her. At last she freed herself, and said shakily, 'All the supper will have gone if we stay out here much longer.'

He tucked her arm through his, clasping his other hand over hers. 'Who needs food when he's with a beautiful woman?'

'Well, *I'm* hungry!' she said firmly, and as she spoke realised that a figure she had dimly been aware of, standing in the doorway and looking out on to the patio, was David. He was back! Her heart leapt with an idiotic joy, then plunged to the depths of despair. David's expression was one of utter contempt as he saw her on Kirk Magnusson's arm. He didn't even speak to them, but turned round and vanished. Jacqui did not see him again.

Kirk said casually, 'Wasn't that David?'

Jacqui's throat was dry. 'Yes.'

'He disappeared suddenly. Like a man who was jealous because his lover was with another man!' He laughed softly and brushed his lips across her cheek. 'Flirting with the opposition too!'

Jacqui felt her cheeks warming, but not from his kiss. 'I shouldn't imagine that was the reason.' And what if it was? That would only be because David might have been expecting to have her to himself for as long as she remained in Maneroo. He was perfectly safe from involvement because she was leaving. Well, she was glad he'd seen her with Kirk. If he had seen Kirk kissing her, all the better, that should convince David that he wasn't special in her life either.

'I wonder if his other little friend's here,' said Kirk as they entered the hall and crossed to the supper tables set up at one end.

Jacqui glanced at him with a querying look.

'Rina Parkinson. Temperamental child. You should see her throw her racket around when she loses! She could be beautiful if she'd stop starving herself. I wonder what the set-up is with her and David. Dutch uncle or sugar-daddy?' He arched an eyebrow. 'Would you know?'

'Dutch uncle, I presume. His parents and hers are friends. He's a great deal older than she is.' Despite what David had told her, Jacqui felt uncomfortable talking about Rina, and the knowledge that in the end he might still marry the girl was more painful than it should have been.

Kirk chuckled as he filled a plate with food and

handed it to her. 'I wonder. She's a sexy little piece. But I suppose Dutch uncles do take their nieces to Melbourne for quite innocent reasons.' Sceptical laughter made his opinion clear.

Jacqui felt her whole body clench. David had taken Rina to Melbourne with him? And hadn't told her that was what he intended. Well, of course not! 'I suppose they do,' she said, concealing her feelings with difficulty. 'How do you know he did, anyway?' she asked, feigning only casual interest.

Kirk's look proved he wasn't fooled. He was enjoying her discomfort. 'I happened to see Rina in town quite early on Monday morning. She was in David's car in the car park waiting for him to come back from doing business with an automatic teller machine. I happened to park alongside. She mentioned they were off to Melbourne again.' His blue eyes mocked her. 'You won't get much change from him, Jacqui,' he said softly.

Jacqui swallowed her food, gulped a cup of coffee and then pleaded a returning headache. Kirk was reluctant to let her go—naturally he wanted to press what he thought was his advantage—but she managed it in the end. She was glad she had come in her own car, so there was no need for him to drive her home. Coping with Kirk in the amorous mood he was in tonight was rather more than she felt capable of doing. It wasn't a lie that her head was aching, it was— pounding with the humiliating knowledge that David had made love to her, had even mentioned that he was going to Melbourne, but not that he was going with Rina. Shades of Carey. . . Maybe all that emotional stuff about Rina had been fictitious after all, just David playing on her sympathy, and at the same time providing a reason to keep her at arm's length.

'I am the world's champion fool,' she told herself.

Jacqui was half inclined not to go to work in the morning. She was even more than half inclined to pack her bags and run. But swinging the lead she had always regarded as tempting fate, and also dishonest. To quit altogether so near to the end of her agreement would be even more dishonest. She couldn't do either. She had to see this through, she told herself. There were only another couple of weeks to go, and then she could take off with Lissa and forget all about Maneroo and the charismatic medical officer at Lakeside Community Hospital. She knew, of course, that she would never entirely forget him.

As usual he arrived on the ward at ten-thirty precisely. He was brisk and impersonal, scarcely looking at Jacqui throughout the round, which to her seemed interminable. With the patients he was bright and breezy, his normal self. If this cold shoulder was because she had been at a tennis dance with Kirk Magnusson, then he really did have a nerve, Jacqui thought. Especially after he'd spent several days away with Rina. Or maybe it was just his way of telling her without words that Sunday had been an aberration and he had no intention of repeating the lapse. Maybe he'd come to the dance last night intending to do that, and Kirk's monopolisation of her had thwarted him.

With all kinds of thoughts chasing around her head, Jacqui found it hard to concentrate, and twice David had to repeat himself when asking her something. At last the round was over and Jacqui returned to her office. She did not expect David to join her for coffee this morning. She paused outside her door.

'Is that everything?' She was chilly, distant.

He shocked her by saying roughly, 'No, it bloody well isn't!'

He practically pushed her into the office and closed the door sharply. Jacqui retreated behind her desk. She had never seen such a grim expression on his face. 'Did you enjoy the tennis club dance last night?' he demanded, dark blue pupils accusing.

'Yes, very much,' she lied. A small pause. 'I hope you and Rina enjoyed your trip to Melbourne.'

He had the grace to look taken aback. 'How do you know I took her to Melbourne?'

'Kirk spoke to her in the car park when she was waiting for you on Monday morning.'

'God! Small towns!' he exclaimed.

'The doctor sneezes and everyone knows about it. Must be awful for you, David.' She couldn't help the sarcasm, or saying, 'That was a lot of fantasy you gave me about her, wasn't it? Just to get my sympathy. You ought to be ashamed. . .'

He came over to her desk and put his palms flat on its surface, leaning towards her. 'Don't you know me better than that?' he said quietly, obviously deeply stung by her words.

Jacqui moistened her lips apprehensively. Was she wrong after all? 'You didn't tell me you were taking her to Melbourne,' she said in a grey little voice.

'I didn't know I would be. I wasn't sure what would happen. I just thought I might. . .' He pushed his hands up through his hair, a sure sign of his agitation. 'Jacqui, everything I told you about Rina is absolutely true. After Sunday morning. . .well, I knew I had to do something drastic. I'd been pussyfooting around for too long. I had to be firm with her. I had to call her bluff.'

'How did you do that?'

'I took your advice! I first made some arrangements with friends of mine in Melbourne, then I tackled Rina. I told her there was no chance I would marry her because. . .'

'Because what?'

'Because I was going to marry you.' Jacqui gasped, but he went on, 'I told her flatly that she must come to terms with it, and that I was arranging for her to stay with friends of mine in Melbourne where she would behave sensibly and this time undergo proper treatment for anorexia, and where she would meet people in her peer group. She wept and wailed and tried every wile she knows, but I stood firm and refused to be intimidated. I don't mind telling you I was worried, but I'm happy to say it worked. I stopped being avuncular and acted like a heavy-handed father. She ended up hating me! She might have tried to give Kirk the wrong impression, but the truth is she was glad to let me drive her to Melbourne and install her with my friends—who have three daughters all a little older than her and much more sophisticated. She won't find them boring. Besides, they all have loads of friends—boys included. I also managed to get her to a psychiatrist. I felt badly about bullying her, but I stuck to my guns, and it worked.'

'You mean she capitulated because you told her you were definitely going to marry someone else?' Jacqui said, seething with outrage at the calm way he had admitted using her. 'But you knew perfectly well you had no intention. . .you *used* me. . .'

Anger flashed in his dark blue eyes as he said, 'I did not! I had every intention of asking you to marry me, and after Sunday I was stupid and egotistical enough to imagine I even had a chance of being accepted, until I saw you in the arms of that smoothie at the tennis club.'

'If you mean Kirk——'

'Of course I mean Magnusson! Or were you necking with a few others besides? There are some fairly charismatic characters around even in Maneroo, and that's the kind of man you go for, isn't it? I met an old mate at South City General while I was in Melbourne, and he told me about you and that Carey Matthews bloke who just got two years for fraud. You were engaged to him, weren't you? I'm surprised you're not engaged to Magnusson by now—he's nearly as devious. He's the guy who hoped to benefit from a hefty kickback over the sale of Lakeside, and get himself elected to the council next election, but maybe you knew that and didn't care, though why you helped the cause, I can't imagine. . .' His brow furrowed in perplexity at this seeming anomaly.

'Can't you?'

He stared at her belligerently. 'You're just like Elise. . .'

Jacqui asked quietly, 'Were you really going to ask me to marry you, David?'

'More fool me!'

'Why were you going to do that?' she persisted on a held breath.

He slammed his fist on her desk, and she prayed no one would come in yet. 'Because on Saturday night I realised how much I loved you, how I didn't want to live without you, and on Sunday morning I still felt the same way. It was no mad impulse. I'd been fighting the feeling for weeks, because you were only here temporarily and would eventually dash off elsewhere or back to Britain. You made it clear you didn't want to get involved. Neither did I at first. I'd had enough humiliation over Elise, and Rina was driving me crazy. But I did get involved. Every damn day I got a little more involved with you, while you sailed blithely along being nice to me but apparently preferring more charismatic types, dubious characters like Kirk Magnusson and this Carey creature——'

Jacqui shouted at him, 'I didn't! I preferred *you*! Oh, this is crazy. David, I hated myself for being fooled by Carey, by the suave, smooth-talking charismatic man who turned out to be so devious. In the beginning, I thought you were that type too. . .'

'Me? I'm not charismatic!' He looked astounded.

Jacqui laughed softly at his amazement. 'Well, you do have a great deal of charm. I was determined not to be taken in again. Carey wasn't just a swindler, he did to me what Elise did to you. He two-timed me and humiliated me. It was his mother who told me he was about to break off our engagement.'

'Is that true?' David seemed stunned.

'Yes. I vowed never to get involved with that kind of man again, but I couldn't stop myself falling in love with you, even when I knew it was futile. You made it very clear that you preferred your freedom, and I thought you were being devious about Rina. . .'

'Did you say you fell in love with me?' David asked in a wondering tone.

'I'm afraid so.'

'You're not joking?'

'I was never more serious in my life.'

He seemed dazed now. 'So on Sunday I wasn't fooling myself?' A smile was struggling on his lips. 'Even after we made love, and I hoped. . . I still wasn't sure the sophisticated city slicker would be interested in marrying a country doctor who doesn't even want a better-paid consultancy in a bigger hospital. . .'

'That's not me! I'm not sophisticated or a city slicker! Well, not any more. . .and I don't care if you want to dig ditches!'

'Jacqui, does this mean you're willing to take a chance on me, despite Carey?' The dark blue eyes were still anxious behind the obvious loving in them.

'I'm more than willing if you are,' Jacqui said in a low voice. 'I promise you I won't treat you the way Elise did, and I don't believe you'd treat me the way Carey did.'

He looked at her steadily for what seemed an interminable moment. At last he murmured, 'Then what are we arguing about?' He rounded the desk and drew her unprotesting into his arms. His mouth met hers with warmth and tenderness and then he smiled into her eyes. 'I don't think we need to dot any more "i"s and cross any more "t"s right now, do we?'

Laughing softly, Jacqui rested her cheek against his chest. 'No.'

'Could you bear living in Maneroo?' he asked anxiously.

'Lately I've been wondering how I could bear to live anywhere else.'

He tilted her chin and kissed her lips. 'Why don't you invite your folks out for the wedding?'

'I was thinking of going home for Christmas, but maybe they could stay on for Christmas too.' And she must persuade Lissa to put off going home until she'd been bridesmaid, Jacqui thought, as happiness welled up inside her.

David stroked her cheek with a tenderness that almost made her weep. 'How am I going to last out this long, long day?' He smoothed her hair. 'How am I going to wait all day to let your beautiful hair down again?'

'I really don't know, Doctor, darling. . .' Jacqui put the pause in the right place and clung to him, dizzy with joy. Vaguely it occurred to her that it was odd that no one had come in during the past twenty minutes or so. Fate must have taken a hand and forestalled all interruptions until everything was solved.

Blissfully, she allowed another two minutes to pass in David's arms, unaware that Angela, who, unnoticed, had looked in earlier and recognised a lovers' quarrel when she saw one, that might yet resolve itself into what she had hoped for but not expected, was the one who had kept people at bay, and who was now looking at her watch and thinking, 'I'll give them two minutes more, that's all!'

2 COMPELLING READS
FOR AUGUST 1990

HONOUR BOUND – Shirley Larson £2.99

The last time Shelly Armstrong had seen Justin Corbett, she'd been a tongue tied teenager overwhelmed by his good looks and opulent lifestyle. Now she was an accomplished pilot with her own flying school, and equal to Justin in all respects but one – she was still a novice at loving.

SUMMER LIGHTNING – Sandra James £2.99

The elemental passions of *Spring Thunder* come alive again in the sequel . . .
Maggie Howard is staunchly against the resumption of logging in her small Oregon town – McBride Lumber had played too often with the lives of families there. So when Jared McBride returned determined to reopen the operation, Maggie was equally determined to block his every move – whatever the cost.

W❤RLDWIDE

Available from Boots, Martins, John Menzies, W.H. Smith, Woolworths and other paperback stockists.

Zodiac Wordsearch
Competition

How would you like a years supply of Mills & Boon Romances ABSOLUTELY FREE?

Well, you can win them! All you have to do is complete the word puzzle below and send it into us by Dec 31st 1990. The first five correct entries picked out of the bag after this date will each win a years supply of Mills & Boon Romances (Six books every month - worth over £100!) What could be easier?

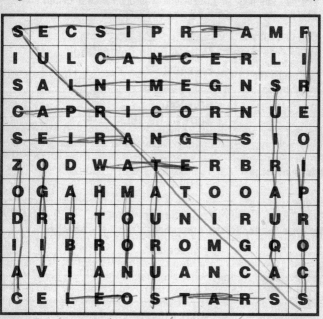

S	E	C	S	I	P	R	I	A	M	F
I	U	L	C	A	N	C	E	R	L	I
S	A	I	N	I	M	E	G	N	S	R
G	A	P	R	I	C	O	R	N	U	E
S	E	I	R	A	N	G	I	S	I	O
Z	O	D	W	A	T	E	R	B	R	I
O	G	A	H	M	A	T	O	O	A	P
D	R	R	T	O	U	N	I	R	U	R
I	I	B	R	O	R	O	M	G	Q	O
A	V	I	A	N	U	A	N	C	A	C
C	E	L	E	O	S	T	A	R	S	S

Pisces ✓ | Aries ✓ | Leo ✓ | Earth ✓
Cancer ✓ | Gemini ✓ | Virgo ✓ | Star ✓
Scorpio ✓ | Taurus ✓ | Fire ✓ | Sign ✓
Aquarius ✓ | Libra ✓ | Water ✓ | Moon ✓
Capricorn ✓ | Sagittarius ✓ | Zodiac ✓ | Air ✓

Please turn over for entry details

How to enter

All the words listed overleaf, below the word puzzle, are hidden in the grid. You can can find them by reading the letters forwards, backwards, up and down, or diagonally. When you find a word, circle it, or put a line through it. After you have found all the words, the left-over letters will spell a secret message that you can read from left to right, from the top of the puzzle through to the bottom.

Don't forget to fill in your name and address in the space provided and pop this page in an envelope (you don't need a stamp) and post it today. Competition closes Dec 31st 1990.

Only one entry per household (more than one will render the entry invalid).

Mills & Boon Competition
Freepost
P.O. Box 236
Croydon
Surrey CR9 9EL

Hidden message _____

_____

Are you a Reader Service subscriber.   Yes ❑   No ❑

Name _____

Address _____

_____

_____

_____ **Postcode** _____

You may be mailed with other offers as a result of entering this competition.
If you would prefer not to be mailed please tick the box. No ❑

COMP9